When I Was a Witch

Charlotte Gilman

The Yellow Wallpaper
First published in 1891
If I Were a Man
First published in 1914
When I Was a Witch
First published in 1910
A Middle-Sized Artist
First published in 1911
Turned
First published in 1911
Her Housekeeper
First published in 1911
Martha's Mother
First published in 1910
Three Thanksgivings
First published in 1909
The Barrel
First published in 1910
Two Storks
First published in 1910
A Coincidence
First published in 1910
While The King Slept
First published in 1910
The Cottagette
First published in 1910
An Offender
First published in 1910
Mr. Grey
First published in 1910
A Word In Season
First published in 1910
My Astonishing Dodo
First published in 1910

ISBN-10: 1546446079
ISBN-13: 978-1546446071

Contents

The Yellow Wallpaper

It is very seldom that mere ordinary people like John and myself secure ancestral halls for the summer. A colonial mansion, a hereditary estate, I would say a haunted house, and reach the height of romantic felicity— but that would be asking too much of fate! Still I will proudly declare that there is something strange about it. Else, why should it be let so cheaply? And why has it stood so long untenanted?

John laughs at me, of course, but one expects that in marriage. John is practical in the extreme. He has no patience with faith, an intense horror of superstition, and he scoffs openly at any talk of things not to be felt and seen and put down in figures. John is a physician, and *perhaps*— (I would not say it to a living soul, of course, but this is dead paper and a great relief to my mind—) *perhaps* that is one reason I do not get well faster.

You see John does not believe I am sick! And what can one do? If a physician of high standing, and one's own husband, assures friends and relatives that there is really nothing the matter with one but temporary nervous depression— a slight hysterical tendency— what is one to do?

My brother is also a physician, and also of high standing, and he says the same thing. So I take phosphates or phosphites— whichever it is, and tonics, and journeys, and air, and exercise, and am absolutely forbidden to "work" until I am well again.

Personally, I disagree with their ideas. Personally, I believe that congenial work, with excitement and change, would do me good. But what is one to do?

I did write for a while in spite of them; but it *does* exhaust me a good deal— having to be so sly about it, or else meet with heavy opposition. I sometimes fancy that in my condition if I had less opposition and more society and stimulus— but John says the very worst thing I can do is to think about my condition, and I confess it always makes me feel bad.

So I will let it alone and talk about the house. The most beautiful place! It is quite alone, standing well back from the road, quite three miles from the village.

It makes me think of English places that you read about, for there are hedges and walls and gates that lock, and lots of separate little houses for the gardeners and people.

There is a *delicious* garden! I never saw such a garden— large and shady, full of box-bordered paths, and lined with long grape-covered arbors with seats under them. There were greenhouses, too, but they are all broken now.

There was some legal trouble, I believe, something about the heirs and coheirs; anyhow, the place has been empty for years. That spoils my ghostliness, I am afraid, but I don't care— there is something strange about the house— I can feel it. I even said so to John one moonlight evening, but he said what I felt was a *draught*, and shut the window.

I get unreasonably angry with John sometimes. I'm sure I never used to be so sensitive. I think it is due to this nervous condition. But John says if I feel so, I shall neglect proper self-control; so I take pains to control myself— before him, at least, and that makes me very tired.

I don't like our room a bit. I wanted one downstairs that opened on the piazza and had roses all over the window, and such pretty old-fashioned chintz hangings! but John would not hear of it. He said there was only one window and not room for two beds, and no near room for him if he took another.

He is very careful and loving, and hardly lets me stir without special direction. I have a schedule prescription for each hour in the day; he takes all care from me, and so I feel basely ungrateful not to value it more. He said we came here solely on my account, that I was to have perfect rest and all the air I could get.

"Your exercise depends on your strength, my dear," said he, "and your food somewhat on your appetite; but air you can absorb all the time." So we took the nursery at the top of the house. It is a big, airy room, the whole floor nearly, with windows that look all ways, and air and sunshine galore. It was nursery first and then playroom and gymnasium, I should judge; for the windows are barred for little children, and there are rings and things in the walls.

The paint and paper look as if a boys' school had used it. It is stripped off— the paper— in great patches all around the head of my bed, about as far as I can reach, and in a great place on the other side of the room low down. I never saw a worse paper in my life. One of those sprawling flamboyant patterns committing every artistic sin. It is dull enough to confuse the eye in following, pronounced enough to constantly irritate and provoke study, and when you follow the lame uncertain curves for a little distance they suddenly commit suicide— plunge off at outrageous angles, destroy themselves in unheard of contradictions.

The color is repellent, almost revolting; a smoldering unclean yellow, strangely faded by the slow-turning sunlight. It is a dull yet lurid orange in some places, a sickly sulfur tint in others. No wonder the children hated it! I should hate it myself if I had to live in this room long.

There comes John, and I must put this away,— he hates to have me write a word.

We have been here two weeks, and I haven't felt like writing before, since that first day. I am sitting by the window now, up in this atrocious nursery, and there is nothing to hinder my writing as much as I please, save lack of strength. John is away all day, and even some nights when his cases are serious. I am glad my case is not serious! But these nervous troubles are dreadfully depressing.

John does not know how much I really suffer. He knows there is no *reason* to suffer, and that satisfies him. Of course it is only nervousness. It does weigh on me so not to do my duty in any way! I meant to be such a help to John, such a real rest and comfort, and here I am a comparative burden already!

Nobody would believe what an effort it is to do what little I am able,— to dress and entertain, and order things. It is fortunate Mary is so good with the baby. Such a dear baby! And yet I *cannot* be with him, it makes me so nervous.

I suppose John never was nervous in his life. He laughs at me so about this wallpaper! At first he meant to re-paper the room, but afterwards he said that I was letting it get the better of me, and that nothing was worse for a nervous patient than to give way to such fancies. He said that after the wallpaper was changed it would be the heavy bedstead, and then the barred windows, and then that gate at the head of the stairs, and so on.

"You know the place is doing you good," he said, "and really, dear, I don't care to renovate the house just for a three months' rental."

"Then do let us go downstairs," I said, "there are such pretty rooms there."

Then he took me in his arms and called me a blessed little goose, and said he would go down to the cellar, if I wished, and have it whitewashed into the bargain. But he is right enough about the beds and windows and things.

3

It is an airy and comfortable room as any one need wish, and, of course, I would not be so silly as to make him uncomfortable just for a whim. I'm really getting quite fond of the big room, all but that horrid paper. Out of one window I can see the garden, those mysterious deep-shaded arbors, the riotous old-fashioned flowers, and bushes and gnarly trees. Out of another I get a lovely view of the bay and a little private wharf belonging to the estate.

There is a beautiful shaded lane that runs down there from the house. I always fancy I see people walking in these numerous paths and arbors, but John has cautioned me not to give way to fancy in the least. He says that with my imaginative power and habit of story-making, a nervous weakness like mine is sure to lead to all manner of excited fancies, and that I ought to use my will and good sense to check the tendency. So I try.

I think sometimes that if I were only well enough to write a little it would relieve the press of ideas and rest me. But I find I get pretty tired when I try.

It is so discouraging not to have any advice and companionship about my work. When I get really well, John says we will ask Cousin Henry and Julia down for a long visit; but he says he would as soon put fireworks in my pillow-case as to let me have those stimulating people about now. I wish I could get well faster. But I must not think about that.

This paper looks to me as if it *knew* what a vicious influence it had! There is a recurrent spot where the pattern lolls like a broken neck and two bulbous eyes stare at you upside down. I get positively angry with the impertinence of it and the everlastingness. Up and down and sideways they crawl, and those absurd, unblinking eyes are everywhere. There is one place where two breadths didn't match, and the eyes go all up and down the line, one a little higher than the other. I never saw so much expression in an inanimate thing before, and we all know how much expression they have!

I used to lie awake as a child and get more entertainment and terror out of blank walls and plain furniture than most children could find in a toy store. I remember what a kindly wink the knobs of our big, old bureau used to have, and there was one chair that always seemed like a strong friend. I used to feel that if any of the other things looked too fierce I could always hop into that chair and be safe.

The furniture in this room is no worse than inharmonious, however, for we had to bring it all from downstairs. I suppose when this was used as a playroom they had to take the nursery things out, and no wonder!

I never saw such ravages as the children have made here. The wallpaper, as I said before, is torn off in spots, and it sticks closer than a brother— they must have had perseverance as well as hatred. Then the floor is scratched and gouged and splintered, the plaster itself is dug out here and there, and this great heavy bed which is all we found in the room, looks as if it had been through the wars. But I don't mind it a bit— only the paper.

There comes John's sister. Such a dear girl as she is, and so careful of me! I must not let her find me writing. She is a perfect and enthusiastic housekeeper, and hopes for no better profession. I verily believe she thinks it is the writing which made me sick! But I can write when she is out, and see her a long way off from these windows. There is one that commands the road, a lovely shaded winding road, and one that just looks off over the country. A lovely country, too, full of great elms and velvet meadows.

This wall-paper has a kind of sub-pattern in a different shade, a particularly irritating one, for you can only see it in certain lights, and not clearly then. But in the places where it isn't faded and where the sun is just so— I can see a strange, provoking, formless sort of figure, that seems to skulk about behind that silly and conspicuous front design. There's sister on the stairs!

Well, the Fourth of July is over! The people are gone and I am tired out. John thought it might do me good to see a little company, so we just had mother and Nellie and the children down for a week. Of course I didn't do a thing. Jennie sees to everything now. But it tired me all the same.

John says if I don't pick up faster he shall send me to Weir Mitchell in the fall. But I don't want to go there at all. I had a friend who was in his hands once, and she says he is just like John and my brother, only more so! Besides, it is such an undertaking to go so far.

I don't feel as if it was worthwhile to turn my hand over for anything, and I'm getting dreadfully fretful and querulous. I cry at nothing, and cry most of the time. Of course I don't when John is here, or anybody else, but when I am alone. And I am alone a good deal just now. John is kept in town very often by serious cases, and Jennie is good and lets me alone when I want her to. So I walk a little in the garden or down that lovely lane, sit on the porch under the roses, and lie down up here a good deal.

I'm getting really fond of the room in spite of the wallpaper. Perhaps *because* of the wallpaper. It dwells in my mind so!

I lie here on this great immovable bed— it is nailed down, I believe— and follow that pattern about by the hour. It is as good as gymnastics, I assure you. I start, we'll say, at the bottom, down in the corner over there where it has not been touched, and I determine for the thousandth time that I *will* follow that pointless pattern to some sort of a conclusion.

I know a little of the principle of design, and I know this thing was not arranged on any laws of radiation, or alternation, or repetition, or symmetry, or anything else that I ever heard of. It is repeated, of course, by the breadths, but not otherwise.

Looked at in one way each breadth stands alone, the bloated curves and flourishes—a kind of "debased Romanesque" with *delirium tremens*— go waddling up and down in isolated columns of fatuity. But, on the other hand, they connect diagonally, and the sprawling outlines run off in great slanting waves of optic horror, like a lot of wallowing seaweeds in full chase.

The whole thing goes horizontally, too, at least it seems so, and I exhaust myself in trying to distinguish the order of its going in that direction. They have used a horizontal breadth for a frieze, and that adds wonderfully to the confusion.

There is one end of the room where it is almost intact, and there, when the cross-lights fade and the low sun shines directly upon it, I can almost fancy radiation after all,— the interminable grotesques seem to form around a common center and rush off in headlong plunges of equal distraction. It makes me tired to follow it. I will take a nap I guess.

I don't know why I should write this. I don't want to. I don't feel able. And I know John would think it absurd. But I *must* say what I feel and think in some way— it is such a relief! But the effort is getting to be greater than the relief.

Half the time now I am awfully lazy, and lie down ever so much. John says I mustn't lose my strength, and has me take cod liver oil and lots of tonics and things, to say nothing of ale and wine and rare meat.

Dear John! He loves me very dearly, and hates to have me sick. I tried to have a real earnest reasonable talk with him the other day, and tell him how I wish he would let me go and make a visit to Cousin Henry and Julia. But he said I wasn't able to go, nor able to stand it after I got there; and I did not make out a very good case for myself, for I was crying before I had finished. It is getting to be a great effort for me to think straight. Just this nervous weakness I suppose.

And dear John gathered me up in his arms, and just carried me upstairs and laid me on the bed, and sat by me and read to me till it tired my head. He said I was his darling and his comfort and all he had, and that I must take care of myself for his sake, and keep well. He says no one but myself can help me out of it, that I must use my will and self-control and not let any silly fancies run away with me.

There's one comfort, the baby is well and happy, and does not have to occupy this nursery with the horrid wall-paper. If we had not used it, that blessed child would have! What a fortunate escape! Why, I wouldn't have a child of mine, an impressionable little thing, live in such a room for worlds. I never thought of it before, but it is lucky that John kept me here after all, I can stand it so much easier than a baby, you see.

Of course I never mention it to them any more— I am too wise,—but I keep watch of it all the same. There are things in that paper that nobody knows but me, or ever will. Behind that outside pattern the dim shapes get clearer every day. It is always the same shape, only very numerous. And it is like a woman stooping down and creeping about behind that pattern. I don't like it a bit. I wonder— I begin to think— I wish John would take me away from here!

It is so hard to talk with John about my case, because he is so wise, and because he loves me so. But I tried it last night. It was moonlight. The moon shines in all around just as the sun does. I hate to see it sometimes, it creeps so slowly, and always comes in by one window or another.

John was asleep and I hated to waken him, so I kept still and watched the moonlight on that undulating wallpaper till I felt creepy. The faint figure behind seemed to shake the pattern, just as if she wanted to get out. I got up softly and went to feel and see if the paper *did* move, and when I came back John was awake.

"What is it, little girl?" he said. "Don't go walking about like that— you'll get cold."

I though it was a good time to talk, so I told him that I really was not gaining here, and that I wished he would take me away.

"Why darling!" said he, "our lease will be up in three weeks, and I can't see how to leave before. The repairs are not done at home, and I cannot possibly leave town just now. Of course if you were in any danger, I could and would, but you really are better, dear, whether you can see it or not. I am a doctor, dear, and I know. You are gaining flesh and color, your appetite is better, I feel really much easier about you."

7

"I don't weigh a bit more," said I, "nor as much; and my appetite may be better in the evening when you are here, but it is worse in the morning when you are away!"

"Bless her little heart!" said he with a big hug, "she shall be as sick as she pleases! But now let's improve the shining hours by going to sleep, and talk about it in the morning!"

"And you won't go away?" I asked gloomily.

"Why, how can I, dear? It is only three weeks more and then we will take a nice little trip of a few days while Jennie is getting the house ready. Really dear you are better!"

"Better in body perhaps—" I began, and stopped short, for he sat up straight and looked at me with such a stern, reproachful look that I could not say another word.

"My darling," said he, "I beg of you, for my sake and for our child's sake, as well as for your own, that you will never for one instant let that idea enter your mind! There is nothing so dangerous, so fascinating, to a temperament like yours. It is a false and foolish fancy. Can you not trust me as a physician when I tell you so?"

So of course I said no more on that score, and we went to sleep before long. He thought I was asleep first, but I wasn't, and lay there for hours trying to decide whether that front pattern and the back pattern really did move together or separately.

On a pattern like this, by daylight, there is a lack of sequence, a defiance of law, that is a constant irritant to a normal mind. The color is hideous enough, and unreliable enough, and infuriating enough, but the pattern is torturing. You think you have mastered it, but just as you get well underway in following, it turns a back— somersault and there you are. It slaps you in the face, knocks you down, and tramples upon you. It is like a bad dream.

The outside pattern is a florid arabesque, reminding one of a fungus. If you can imagine a toadstool in joints, an interminable string of toadstools, budding and sprouting in endless convolutions— why, that is something like it. That is, sometimes!

There is one marked peculiarity about this paper, a thing nobody seems to notice but myself, and that is that it changes as the light changes. When the sun shoots in through the east window— I always watch for that first long, straight ray— it changes so quickly that I never can quite believe it. That is why I watch it always.

By moonlight— the moon shines in all night when there is a moon— I wouldn't know it was the same paper.

At night in any kind of light, in twilight, candle light, lamplight, and worst of all by moonlight, it becomes bars! The outside pattern I mean, and the woman behind it is as plain as can be.

I didn't realize for a long time what the thing was that showed behind, that dim sub-pattern, but now I am quite sure it is a woman. By daylight she is subdued, quiet. I fancy it is the pattern that keeps her so still. It is so puzzling. It keeps me quiet by the hour.

I lie down ever so much now. John says it is good for me, and to sleep all I can. Indeed he started the habit by making me lie down for an hour after each meal. It is a very bad habit I am convinced, for you see I don't sleep. And that cultivates deceit, for I don't tell them I'm awake— O no!

The fact is I am getting a little afraid of John. He seems very strange sometimes, and even Jennie has an inexplicable look. It strikes me occasionally, just as a scientific hypothesis,— that perhaps it is the paper!

I have watched John when he did not know I was looking, and come into the room suddenly on the most innocent excuses, and I've caught him several times *looking at the paper!*

And Jennie too. I caught Jennie with her hand on it once. She didn't know I was in the room, and when I asked her in a quiet, a very quiet voice, with the most restrained manner possible, what she was doing with the paper— she turned around as if she had been caught stealing, and looked quite angry— asked me why I should frighten her so! Then she said that the paper stained everything it touched, that she had found yellow smooches on all my clothes and John's, and she wished we would be more careful!

Did not that sound innocent? But I know she was studying that pattern, and I am determined that nobody shall find it out but myself!

Life is very much more exciting now than it used to be. You see I have something more to expect, to look forward to, to watch. I really do eat better, and am more quiet than I was. John is so pleased to see me improve! He laughed a little the other day, and said I seemed to be flourishing in spite of my wallpaper.

I turned it off with a laugh. I had no intention of telling him it was *because* of the wallpaper— he would make fun of me. He might even want to take me away. I don't want to leave now until I have found it out. There is a week more, and I think that will be enough.

I'm feeling ever so much better! I don't sleep much at night, for it is so interesting to watch developments; but I sleep a good deal in the daytime.

In the daytime it is tiresome and perplexing. There are always new shoots on the fungus, and new shades of yellow all over it. I cannot keep count of them, though I have tried conscientiously. It is the strangest yellow, that wallpaper! It makes me think of all the yellow things I ever saw— not beautiful ones like buttercups, but old foul, bad yellow things.

But there is something else about that paper— the smell! I noticed it the moment we came into the room, but with so much air and sun it was not bad. Now we have had a week of fog and rain, and whether the windows are open or not, the smell is here. It creeps all over the house. I find it hovering in the dining-room, skulking in the parlor, hiding in the hall, lying in wait for me on the stairs.

It gets into my hair. Even when I go to ride, if I turn my head suddenly and surprise it— there is that smell! Such a peculiar odor, too! I have spent hours in trying to analyze it, to find what it smelled like. It is not bad— at first, and very gentle, but quite the subtlest, most enduring odor I ever met.

In this damp weather it is awful, I wake up in the night and find it hanging over me. It used to disturb me at first. I thought seriously of burning the house— to reach the smell. But now I am used to it. The only thing I can think of that it is like is the *color* of the paper! A yellow smell.

There is a very funny mark on this wall, low down, near the mop-board. A streak that runs round the room. It goes behind every piece of furniture, except the bed, a long, straight, even *smooch*, as if it had been rubbed over and over. I wonder how it was done and who did it, and what they did it for. Round and round and round— round and round and round— it makes me dizzy!

I really have discovered something at last. Through watching so much at night, when it changes so, I have finally found out. The front pattern *does* move— and no wonder! The woman behind shakes it!

Sometimes I think there are a great many women behind, and sometimes only one, and she crawls around fast, and her crawling shakes it all over. Then in the very bright spots she keeps still, and in the very shady spots she just takes hold of the bars and shakes them hard.

And she is all the time trying to climb through. But nobody could climb through that pattern— it strangles so; I think that is why it has so many heads. They get through, and then the pattern strangles them off and turns them upside down, and makes their eyes white! If those heads were covered or taken off it would not be half so bad.

I think that woman gets out in the daytime! And I'll tell you why— privately— I've seen her! I can see her out of every one of my windows! It is the same woman, I know, for she is always creeping, and most women do not creep by daylight.

I see her on that long road under the trees, creeping along, and when a carriage comes she hides under the blackberry vines. I don't blame her a bit. It must be very humiliating to be caught creeping by daylight!

I always lock the door when I creep by daylight. I can't do it at night, for I know John would suspect something at once. And John is so strange now, that I don't want to irritate him. I wish he would take another room! Besides, I don't want anybody to get that woman out at night but myself.

I often wonder if I could see her out of all the windows at once. But, turn as fast as I can, I can only see out of one at one time. And though I always see her, she *may* be able to creep faster than I can turn!

I have watched her sometimes away off in the open country, creeping as fast as a cloud shadow in a high wind.

If only that top pattern could be gotten off from the under one! I mean to try it, little by little.

I have found out another funny thing, but I shan't tell it this time! It does not do to trust people too much.

There are only two more days to get this paper off, and I believe John is beginning to notice. I don't like the look in his eyes. And I heard him ask Jennie a lot of professional questions about me. She had a very good report to give. She said I slept a good deal in the daytime.

John knows I don't sleep very well at night, for all I'm so quiet He asked me all sorts of questions, too, and pretended to be very loving and kind. As if I couldn't see through him!

Still, I don't wonder he acts so, sleeping under this paper for three months. It only interests me, but I feel sure John and Jennie are secretly affected by it.

Hurrah! This is the last day, but it is enough. John is to stay in town over night, and won't be out until this evening. Jennie wanted to sleep with me— the sly thing! but I told her I should undoubtedly rest better for a night all alone. That was clever, for really I wasn't alone a bit!

As soon as it was moonlight and that poor thing began to crawl and shake the pattern, I got up and ran to help her. I pulled and she shook, I shook and she pulled, and before morning we had peeled off yards of that paper. A strip about as high as my head and half around the room. And then when the sun came and that awful pattern began to laugh at me, I declared I would finish it today!

We go away tomorrow, and they are moving all my furniture down again to leave things as they were before. Jennie looked at the wall in amazement, but I told her merrily that I did it out of pure spite at the vicious thing. She laughed and said she wouldn't mind doing it herself, but I must not get tired.

How she betrayed herself that time! But I am here, and no person touches this paper but me— not *alive!*

She tried to get me out of the room— it was too patent! But I said it was so quiet and empty and clean now that I believed I would lie down again and sleep all I could; and not to wake me even for dinner— I would call when I woke. So now she is gone, and the servants are gone, and the things are gone, and there is nothing left but that great bedstead nailed down, with the canvas mattress we found on it.

We shall sleep downstairs tonight, and take the boat home tomorrow. I quite enjoy the room, now it is bare again. How those children did tear about here! This bedstead is fairly gnawed! But I must get to work.

I have locked the door and thrown the key down into the front path. I don't want to go out, and I don't want to have anybody come in, till John comes. I want to astonish him.

I've got a rope up here that even Jennie did not find. If that woman does get out, and tries to get away, I can tie her! But I forgot I could not reach far without anything to stand on! This bed will *not* move! I tried to lift and push it until I was lame, and then I got so angry I bit off a little piece at one corner— but it hurt my teeth.

Then I peeled off all the paper I could reach standing on the floor. It sticks horribly and the pattern just enjoys it! All those strangled heads and bulbous eyes and waddling fungus growths just shriek with derision!

I am getting angry enough to do something desperate. To jump out of the window would be admirable exercise, but the bars are too strong even to try. Besides I wouldn't do it. Of course not. I know well enough that a step like that is improper and might be misconstrued.

I don't like to *look* out of the windows even— there are so many of those creeping women, and they creep so fast. I wonder if they all come out of that wallpaper as I did? But I am securely fastened now by my well-hidden rope— you don't get *me* out in the road there!

I suppose I shall have to get back behind the pattern when it comes night, and that is hard! It is so pleasant to be out in this great room and creep around as I please!

I don't want to go outside. I won't, even if Jennie asks me to. For outside you have to creep on the ground, and everything is green instead of yellow. But here I can creep smoothly on the floor, and my shoulder just fits in that long smooch around the wall, so I cannot lose my way.

Why there's John at the door! It is no use, young man, you can't open it! How he does call and pound! Now he's crying for an axe. It would be a shame to break down that beautiful door!

"John dear!" said I in the gentlest voice, "the key is down by the front steps, under a plantain leaf!"

That silenced him for a few moments. Then he said— very quietly indeed, "Open the door, my darling!"

"I can't," said I. "The key is down by the front door under a plantain leaf!" And then I said it again, several times, very gently and slowly, and said it so often that he had to go and see, and he got it of course, and came in. He stopped short by the door.

"What is the matter?" he cried. "For God's sake, what are you doing!"

I kept on creeping just the same, but I looked at him over my shoulder.

"I've got out at last," said I, "in spite of you and Jane. And I've pulled off most of the paper, so you can't put me back!"

Now why should that man have fainted? But he did, and right across my path by the wall, so that I had to creep over him every time!

* * * * *

Charlotte Gilman

If I Were a Man

Mollie was "true to type." She was a beautiful instance of what is reverentially called "a true woman." Little, of course; no true woman may be big. Pretty, of course; no true woman could possibly be plain. Whimsical, capricious, charming changeable, devoted to pretty clothes and always "wearing them well," as the esoteric phrase has it. (This does not refer to the clothes, they do not wear well in the least, but to some special grace of putting them on and carrying them about, granted to but few, it appears.)

She was also a loving wife and a devoted mother possessed of "the social gift" and the love of "society" that goes with it, and with all these was fond and proud of her home and managed it as capably as— well, as most women do.

If ever there was a true woman it was Mollie Mathewson, yet she was wishing heart and soul she was a man. And all of a sudden she was! She was Gerald, walking down the path so erect and square-shouldered, in a hurry for his morning train, as usual, and, it must be confessed, in something of a temper. . . .

A man! Really a man, with only enough subconscious memory of herself remaining to make her recognize the differences.

At first there was a funny sense of size and weight and extra thickness, the feet and hands seemed strangely large, and her long, straight, free legs swung forward at a gait that made her feel as if on stilts. This soon passed, and in its place, growing all day, wherever she went, came a new and delightful feeling of being the right size.

Everything fitted now. Her back snugly against the seat-back, her feet comfortably on the floor. Her feet? . . . His feet! She studied them carefully. Never before, since her early school days, had she felt such freedom and comfort as to feet. They were firm and solid on the ground when she walked; quick, springy, safe— as when, moved by an unrecognizable impulse, she had run after, caught, and swung aboard the car.

Another impulse fished in a convenient pocket for change-instantly, automatically bringing forth a nickel for the conductor and a penny for the newsboy. These pockets came as a revelation. Of course she had known they were there, had counted them, made fun of them, mended them, even envied them; but she never had dreamed of how it felt to have pockets.

Behind her newspaper she let her consciousness, that odd mingled consciousness, rove from pocket to pocket, realizing the armored assurance of having all those things at hand, instantly get-at-able, ready to meet emergencies.

The cigar case gave her a warm feeling of comfort— it was full; the firmly held fountain pen, safe unless she stood on her head; the keys, pencils, letters, documents, notebook, checkbook, bill folder— all at once, with a deep rushing sense of power and pride, she felt what she had never felt before in all her life— the possession of money, of her own earned money— hers to give or to withhold, not to beg for, tease for, wheedle for— hers. . . .

When he took his train, his seat in the smoking car, she had a new surprise. All about him were the other men, commuters too, and many of them friends of his. To her, they would have been distinguished as "Mary Wade's husband," "the man Belle Grant is engaged to," "that rich Mr. Shopworth," or "that pleasant Mr. Beale." And they would all have lifted their hats to her, bowed, made polite conversation if near enough, especially Mr. Beale.

Now came the feeling of open-eyed acquaintance, of knowing men— as they were. The mere amount of this knowledge was a surprise to her. The whole background of talk from boyhood up, the gossip of barber-shop and club, the conversation of morning and evening hours on trains, the knowledge of political affiliation, of business standing and prospects, of character; in a light she had never known before.

They came and talked to Gerald, one and another. He seemed quite popular. And as they talked, with this new memory and new understanding, an understanding which seemed to include all these men's minds, there poured in on the submerged consciousness beneath a new, a startling knowledge— what men really think of women.

Good, average, American men were there; married men for the most part, and happy, as happiness goes in general. In the minds of each and all there seemed to be a two-story department, quite apart from the rest of their ideas, a separate place where they kept their thoughts and feelings about women.

In the upper half were the tenderest emotions, the most exquisite ideals, the sweetest memories, all lovely sentiments as to "home" and "mother," all delicate admiring adjectives, a sort of sanctuary, where a veiled statue, blindly adored, shared place with beloved yet commonplace experiences.

In the lower half— here that buried consciousness woke to keen distress— they kept quite another assortment of ideas. Here, even in this clean-minded husband of hers, was the memory of stories told at men's dinners, of worse ones overheard in street or car, of base traditions, coarse epithets, gross experiences— known, though not shared. And all these in the department "woman," while in the rest of the mind— here was new knowledge indeed.

The world opened before her. Not the world she had been reared in, where Home had covered all the map, almost, and the rest had been "foreign," or "unexplored country," but the world as it was; man's world, as made, lived in, and seen, by men.

It was dizzying. To see the houses that fled so fast across the car window, in terms of builders' bills, or of some technical insight into materials and methods; to see a passing village with lamentable knowledge of who "owned it" and of how its Boss was rapidly aspiring in state power, or of how that kind of paving was a failure; to see shops, not as mere exhibitions of desirable objects, but as business ventures, many were sinking ships, some promising a profitable voyage. This new world bewildered her.

She, as Gerald, had already forgotten about that bill, over which she, as Mollie, was still crying at home. Gerald was "talking business" with this man, "talking politics" with that, and now sympathizing with the carefully withheld troubles of a neighbor. Mollie had always sympathized with the neighbor's wife before.

She began to struggle violently with this large dominant masculine consciousness. She remembered with sudden clearness things she had read, lectures she had heard, and resented with increasing intensity this serene masculine preoccupation with the male point of view.

Mr. Miles, the little fussy man who lived on the other side of the street, was talking now. He had a large complacent wife; Mollie had never liked her much, but had always thought him rather nice. He was so punctilious in small courtesies. And here he was talking to Gerald— such talk!

"Had to come in here," he said. "Gave my seat to a dame who was bound to have it. There's nothing they won't get when they make up their minds to it— eh?"

"No fear!" said the big man in the next seat. "They haven't much mind to make up, you know, and if they do, they'll change it."

"The real danger," began the Rev. Alfred Smythe, the new Episcopal clergyman, a thin, nervous, tall man with a face several centuries behind the times, "is that they will overstep the limits of their God-appointed sphere."

"Their natural limits ought to hold them, I think," said cheerful Dr. Jones. "You can't get around physiology, I tell you."

"I've never seen any limits, myself, not to what they want, anyhow," said Mr. Miles.

"Merely a rich husband and a fine house and no end of bonnets and dresses, and the latest thing in motors, and a few diamonds, and so on. Keeps us pretty busy."

There was a tired gray man across the aisle. He had a very nice wife, always beautifully dressed, and three unmarried daughters, also beautifully dressed, Mollie knew them. She knew he worked hard, too, and she looked at him now a little anxiously. But she smiled cheerfully.

"Do you good, Miles," he said. "What else would a man work for? A good woman is about the best thing on earth."

"And a bad one's the worse, that's sure," responded Miles.

"She's a pretty weak sister, viewed professionally," Dr. Jones averred with solemnity, and the Rev. Alfred Smythe added, "She brought evil into the world."

Gerald Mathewson sat up straight. Something was stirring in him which he did not recognize, yet could not resist.

"Seems to me we all talk like Noah," he suggested dryly. "or the ancient Hindu scriptures. Women have their limitations, but so do we, God knows. Haven't we known girls in school and college just as smart as we were?"

"They cannot play our games," coldly replied the clergyman.

Gerald measured his meager proportions with a practiced eye.

"I never was particularly good at football myself," he modestly admitted, "but I've known women who could outlast a man in all-round endurance. Besides— life isn't spent in athletics!"

This was sadly true. They all looked down the aisle where a heavy ill-dressed man with a bad complexion sat alone. He had held the top of the columns once, with headlines and photographs. Now he earned less than any of them. . . .

"Yes, we blame them for grafting on us, but are we willing to let our wives work? We are not. It hurts our pride, that's all. We are always criticizing them for making mercenary marriages, but what do we call a girl who marries a chump with no money? Just a poor fool, that's all. And they know it."

"As for Mother Eve, I wasn't there and can't deny the story, but I will say this. If she brought evil into the world, we men have had the lion's share of keeping it going ever since. How about that?"

They drew into the city, and all day long in his business, Gerald was vaguely conscious of new views, strange feelings, and the submerged Mollie learned and learned.

* * * * *

Charlotte Gilman

When I Was a Witch

If I had understood the terms of that one-sided contract with Satan, the Time of Witching would have lasted longer– you may be sure of that. But how was I to tell? It just happened, and has never happened again, though I've tried the same preliminaries as far as I could control them.

The thing began all of a sudden, one October midnight– the 30th, to be exact. It had been hot, really hot, all day, and was sultry and thunderous in the evening; no air stirring, and the whole house stewing with that ill-advised activity which always seems to move the steam radiator when it isn't wanted.

I was in a state of simmering rage– hot enough, even without the weather and the furnace– and I went up on the roof to cool off. A top-floor apartment has that advantage, among others– you can take a walk without the mediation of an elevator boy!

There are things enough in New York to lose one's temper over at the best of times, and on this particular day they seemed to all happen at once, and some fresh ones. The night before, cats and dogs had broken my rest, of course. My morning paper was more than usually mendacious; and my neighbor's morning paper– more visible than my own as I went down town– was more than usually salacious. My cream wasn't cream, and my egg was a relic of the past. My "new" napkins were giving out.

Being a woman, I'm supposed not to swear; but when the motorman disregarded my plain signal, and grinned as he rushed by; when the subway guard waited till I was just about to step on board and then slammed the door in my face, standing behind it calmly for some minutes before the bell rang to warrant his closing, I desired to swear like a mule-driver.

At night it was worse. The way people paw one's back in the crowd! The cow-puncher who packs the people in or jerks them out, the men who smoke and spit, law or no law, the women whose saw-edged cartwheel hats, swashing feathers and deadly pins, add so to one's comfort inside.

Well, as I said, I was in a particularly bad temper, and went up on the roof to cool off. Heavy black clouds hung low overhead, and lightning flickered threateningly here and there.

21

A starved, black cat stole from behind a chimney and mewed dolefully. Poor thing! She had been scalded. The street was quiet for New York. I leaned over a little and looked up and down the long parallels of twinkling lights. A belated cab drew near, the horse so tired he could hardly hold his head up. Then the driver, with a skill born of plenteous practice, flung out his long-lashed whip and curled it under the poor beast's belly with a stinging cut that made me shudder. The horse shuddered too, poor wretch, and jingled his harness with an effort at a trot.

I leaned over the parapet and watched that man with a spirit of unmitigated ill-will. "I wish," said I, slowly– and I did wish it with all my heart– "that every person who strikes or otherwise hurts a horse unnecessarily, shall feel the pain intended– and the horse not feel it!"

It did me good to say it, anyhow, but I never expected any result. I saw the man swing his great whip again, and lay on heartily. I saw him throw up his hands, heard him scream, but I never thought what the matter was, even then.

The lean, black cat, timid but trustful, rubbed against my skirt and mewed. "Poor Kitty" I said; "poor Kitty! It is a shame!" And I thought tenderly of all the thousands of hungry, hunted cats who stink and suffer in this great city.

Later, when I tried to sleep, and up across the stillness rose the raucous shrieks of some of these same sufferers, my pity turned cold.

"Any fool that will try to keep a cat in a city!" I muttered, angrily. Another yell, a pause, an ear-torturing, continuous cry. "I wish," I burst forth, "that every cat in the city was comfortably dead!" A sudden silence fell, and in course of time I got to sleep.

Things went fairly well next morning, till I tried another egg. They were expensive eggs, too.

"I can't help it!" said my sister, who keeps house.

"I know you can't," I admitted. "But somebody could help it. I wish the people who are responsible had to eat their old eggs, and never get a good one till they sold good ones!"

"They'd stop eating eggs, that's all," said my sister, "and eat meat."

"Let them eat meat!" I said, recklessly. "The meat is as bad as the eggs! It's so long since we've had a clean, fresh chicken that I've forgotten how they taste!"

"It's cold storage," said my sister. She is a peaceable sort; I'm not.

"Yes, cold storage!" I snapped. "It ought to be a blessing to tide over shortages, equalize supplies, and lower prices. What does it do? Corner the market, raise prices the year round, and make all the food bad!"

My anger rose. "If there was any way of getting at them!" I cried. "The law don't touch them. They need to be cursed somehow! I'd like to do it! I wish the whole crowd that profit by this vicious business might taste their bad meat, their old fish, their stale milk– whatever they ate. Yes, and feel the prices as we do!"

"They couldn't you know; they're rich," said my sister.

"I know that," I admitted, sulkily. "There's no way of getting at them. But I wish they could. And I wish they knew how people hated them, and felt that, too– till they mended their ways!"

When I left for my office I saw a funny thing. A man who drove a garbage cart took his horse by the bits and jerked and wrenched brutally. I was amazed to see him clap his hands to his own jaws with a moan, while the horse philosophically licked his chops and looked at him.

The man seemed to resent his expression, and struck him on the head, only to rub his own poll and swear amazedly, looking around to see who had hit him.

The horse advanced a step, stretching a hungry nose toward a garbage pail crowned with cabbage leaves, and the man, recovering his sense of proprietorship, swore at him and kicked him in the ribs. That time he had to sit down, turning pale and weak. I watched with growing wonder and delight.

A market wagon came clattering down the street; the hard-faced young ruffian fresh for his morning task. He gathered the ends of the reins and brought them down on the horse's back with a resounding thwack. The horse did not notice this at all, but the boy did. He yelled!

I came to a place where many teamsters were at work hauling dirt and crushed stone. A strange silence and peace hung over the scene where usually the sound of the lash and sight of brutal blows made me hurry by. The men were talking together a little, and seemed to be exchanging notes. It was too good to be true.

I gazed and marveled, waiting for my car. It came, merrily running along. It was not full. There was one not far ahead, which I had missed in watching the horses; there was no other near it in the rear. Yet the coarse-faced person in authority who ran it, went gaily by without stopping, though I stood on the track almost, and waved my umbrella.

23

A hot flush of rage surged to my face. "I wish you felt the blow you deserve," said I, viciously, looking after the car. "I wish you'd have to stop, and back to here, and open the door and apologize. I wish that would happen to all of you, every time you play that trick."

To my infinite amazement, that car stopped and backed till the front door was before me. The motorman opened it. holding his hand to his cheek. "Beg your pardon, madam!" he said.

I passed in, dazed, overwhelmed. Could it be? Could it possibly be that– that what I wished came true. The idea sobered me, but I dismissed it with a scornful smile. "No such luck!" said I.

Opposite me sat a person in petticoats. She was of a sort I particularly detest. No real body of bones and muscles, but the contours of grouped sausages. Complacent, gaudily dressed, heavily wigged and ratted, with powder and perfume and flowers and jewels– and a dog. A poor, wretched, little, artificial dog– alive, but only so by virtue of man's insolence; not a real creature that God made. And the dog had clothes on– and a bracelet! His fitted jacket had a pocket– and a pocket-handkerchief! He looked sick and unhappy.

I meditated on his pitiful position, and that of all the other poor chained prisoners, leading unnatural lives of enforced celibacy, cut off from sunlight, fresh air, the use of their limbs; led forth at stated intervals by unwilling servants, to defile our streets; over-fed, under-exercised, nervous and unhealthy.

"And we say we love them!" said I, bitterly to myself. "No wonder they bark and howl and go mad. No wonder they have almost as many diseases as we do! I wish–" Here the thought I had dismissed struck me again. "I wish that all the unhappy dogs in cities would die at once!" I watched the sad-eyed little invalid across the car. He dropped his head and died. She never noticed it till she got off; then she made fuss enough.

The evening papers were full of it. Some sudden pestilence had struck both dogs and cats, it would appear. Red headlines struck the eye, big letters, and columns were filled out of the complaints of those who had lost their "pets," of the sudden labors of the board of health, and interviews with doctors.

All day, as I went through the office routine, the strange sense of this new power struggled with reason and common knowledge. I even tried a few furtive test "wishes"– wished that the waste basket would fall over, that the inkstand would fill itself; but they didn't.

I dismissed the idea as pure foolishness, till I saw those newspapers, and heard people telling worse stories. One thing I decided at once; not to tell a soul. "Nobody would believe me if I did," said I to myself. "And I won't give them the chance. I've scored on cats and dogs, anyhow– and horses."

As I watched the horses at work that afternoon, and thought of all their unknown sufferings from crowded city stables, bad air and insufficient food, and from the wearing strain of asphalt pavements in wet and icy weather, I decided to have another try on horses.

"I wish," said I, slowly and carefully, but with a fixed intensity of purposes, "that every horse owner, keeper, hirer and driver or rider, might feel what the horse feels, when he suffers at our hands. Feel it keenly and constantly till the case is mended."

I wasn't able to verify this attempt for some time; but the effect was so general that it got widely talked about soon; and this "new wave of humane feeling" soon raised the status of horses in our city. Also it diminished their numbers. People began to prefer motor drays– which was a mighty good thing.

Now I felt pretty well assured in my own mind, and kept my assurance to my self. Also I began to make a list of my cherished grudges, with a fine sense of power and pleasure.

"I must be careful," I said to myself; "very careful; and, above all things, make the punishment fit the crime."

The subway crowding came to my mind next; both the people who crowd because they have to, and the people who make them. "I mustn't punish anybody, for what they can't help," I mused. "But when it's pure meanness!" Then I bethought me of the remote stockholders, of the more immediate directors, of the painfully prominent officials and insolent employees– and got to work.

"I might as well make a good job of it while this lasts," said I to myself. "It's quite a responsibility, but lots of fun." And I wished that every person responsible for the condition of our subways might be mysteriously compelled to ride up and down in them continuously during rush hours. This experiment I watched with keen interest, but for the life of me I could see little difference. There were a few more well-dressed persons in the crowds, that was all. So I came to the conclusion that the general public was mostly to blame, and carried their daily punishment without knowing it.

For the insolent guards and cheating ticket-sellers who give you short change, very slowly, when you are dancing on one foot and your train is there, I merely wished that they might feel the pain their victims would like to give them, short of real injury. They did, I guess.

Then I wished similar things for all manner of corporations and officials. It worked. It worked amazingly. There was a sudden conscientious revival all over the country. The dry bones rattled and sat up. Boards of directors, having troubles enough of their own, were aggravated by innumerable communications from suddenly sensitive stockholders.

In mills and mints and railroads, things began to mend. The country buzzed. The papers fattened. The churches sat up and took credit to themselves. I was incensed at this; and, after brief consideration, wished that every minister would preach to his congregation exactly what he believed and what he thought of them.

I went to six services the next Sunday– about ten minutes each, for two sessions. It was most amusing. A thousand pulpits were emptied forthwith, refilled, re-emptied, and so on, from week to week.

People began to go to church; men largely– women didn't like it as well. They had always supposed the ministers thought more highly of them than now appeared to be the case.

One of my oldest grudges was against the sleeping-car people; and now I began to consider them. How often I had grinned and borne it– with other thousands– submitting helplessly. Here is a railroad– a common carrier– and you have to use it. You pay for your transportation, a good round sum. Then if you wish to stay in the sleeping car during the day, they charge you another two dollars and a half for the privilege of sitting there, whereas you have paid for a seat when you bought your ticket. That seat is now sold to another person– twice sold!

Five dollars for twenty-four hours in a space six feet by three by three at night, and one seat by day; twenty-four of these privileges to a car– $120 a day for the rent of the car– and the passengers to pay the porter besides. That makes $44,800 a year. Sleeping cars are expensive to build, they say. So are hotels; but they do not charge at such a rate. Now, what could I do to get even? Nothing could ever put back the dollars into the millions of pockets; but it might be stopped now, this beautiful process.

So I wished that all persons who profited by this performance might feel a shame so keen that they would make public avowal and apology, and, as partial restitution, offer their wealth to promote the cause of free railroads!

Then I remembered parrots. This was lucky, for my wrath flamed again. It was really cooling, as I tried to work out responsibility and adjust penalties. But parrots! Any person who wants to keep a parrot should go and live on an island alone with their preferred conversationalist!

There was a huge, squawky parrot right across the street from me, adding its senseless, rasping cries to the more necessary evils of other noises. I had also an aunt with a parrot. She was a wealthy, ostentatious person, who had been an only child and inherited her money. Uncle Joseph hated the yelling bird, but that didn't make any difference to Aunt Mathilda. I didn't like this aunt, and wouldn't visit her, lest she think I was truckling for the sake of her money; but after I had wished this time, I called at the time set for my curse to work; and it did work with a vengeance.

There sat poor Uncle Joe, looking thinner and meeker than ever; and my aunt, like an overripe plum, complacent enough.

"Let me out!" said Polly, suddenly. "Let me out to take a walk!"

"The clever thing!" said Aunt Mathilda. "He never said that before."

She let him out. Then he flapped up on the chandelier and sat among the prisms, quite safe.

"What an old pig you are, Mathilda!" said the parrot.

She started to her feet– naturally.

"Born a Pig, trained a Pig, a Pig by nature and education!" said the parrot.

"Nobody would put up with you, except for your money; unless it's this long-suffering husband of yours. He wouldn't, if he hadn't the patience of Job!"

"Hold your tongue!" screamed Aunt Mathilda. "Come down from there! Come here!"

Polly cocked his head and jingled the prisms. "Sit down, Mathilda!" he said, cheerfully. "You've got to listen. You are fat and homely and selfish. You are a nuisance to everybody about you. You have got to feed me and take care of me better than ever– and you've got to listen to me when I talk. Pig!"

I visited another person with a parrot the next day. She put a cloth over his cage when I came in.

"Take it off!" said Polly. She took it off.

"Won't you come into the other room?" she asked me, nervously.

"Better stay here!" said her pet. "Sit still– sit still!"

She sat still.

"Your hair is mostly false," said pretty Poll. "And your teeth– and your outlines. You eat too much. You are lazy. You ought to exercise, and don't know enough. Better apologize to this lady for backbiting! You've got to listen."

The trade in parrots fell off from that day; they say there is no call for them. But the people who kept parrots, keep them yet– parrots live a long time.

Bores were a class of offenders against whom I had long borne undying enmity. Now I rubbed my hands and began on them, with this simple wish: That every person whom they bored should tell them the plain truth.

There is one man whom I have specially in mind. He was blackballed at a pleasant club, but continues to go there. He isn't a member– he just goes; and no one does anything to him. It was very funny after this. He appeared that very night at a meeting, and almost every person present asked him how he came there. "You're not a member, you know," they said. "Why do you butt in? Nobody likes you."

Some were more lenient with him. "Why don't you learn to be more considerate of others, and make some real friends?" they said. "To have a few friends who do enjoy your visits ought to be pleasanter than being a public nuisance."

He disappeared from that club, anyway.

I began to feel very cocky indeed.

In the food business there was already a marked improvement; and in transportation. The hubbub of reformation waxed louder daily, urged on by the unknown sufferings of all the profiters by iniquity. The papers thrived on all this; and as I watched the loud-voiced protestations of my pet abomination in journalism, I had a brilliant idea, literally.

Next morning I was down town early, watching the men open their papers. My abomination was shamefully popular, and never more so than this morning. Across the top was printing in gold letters:

All intentional lies, in adv., editorial, news, or any other
column. . .Scarlet
All malicious matter. . .Crimson
All careless or ignorant mistakes. . .Pink
All for direct self-interest of owner. . .Dark green
All mere bait–to sell the paper. . .Bright green
All advertising, primary or secondary. . .Brown
All sensational and salacious matter. . .Yellow

All hired hypocrisy. . .Purple
Good fun, instruction and entertainment. . .Blue
True and necessary news and honest editorials. . .Ordinary print

You never saw such a crazy quilt of a paper. They were bought like hot cakes for some days; but the real business fell off very soon. They'd have stopped it all if they could; but the papers looked all right when they came off the press. The color scheme flamed out only to the bona-fide reader.

I let this work for about a week, to the immense joy of all the other papers; and then turned it on to them, all at once. Newspaper reading became very exciting for a little, but the trade fell off. Even newspaper editors could not keep on feeding a market like that. The blue printed and ordinary printed matter grew from column to column and page to page. Some papers– small, to be sure, but refreshing– began to appear in blue and black alone. This kept me interested and happy for quite a while; so much so that I quite forgot to be angry at other things.

There was such a change in all kinds of business, following the mere printing of truth in the newspapers. It began to appear as if we had lived in a sort of delirium– not really knowing the facts about anything. As soon as we really knew the facts, we began to behave very differently, of course.

What really brought all my enjoyment to an end was women. Being a woman, I was naturally interested in them, and could see some things more clearly than men could. I saw their real power, their real dignity, their real responsibility in the world; and then the way they dress and behave used to make me fairly frantic. It was like seeing archangels playing jackstraws– or real horses only used as rocking-horses. So I determined to get after them.

How to manage it! What to hit first! Their hats, their ugly, inane, outrageous hats– that is what one thinks of first. Their silly, expensive clothes– their diddling beads and jewelry– their greedy childishness– mostly of the women provided for by rich men.

Then I thought of all the other women, the real ones, the vast majority, patiently doing the work of servants without even a servant's pay, and neglecting the noblest duties of motherhood in favor of house-service; the greatest power on earth, blind, chained, untaught, in a treadmill. I thought of what they might do, compared to what they did do, and my heart swelled with something that was far from anger.

Then I wished– with all my strength– that women, all women, might realize Womanhood at last; its power and pride and place in life; that they might see their duty as mothers of the world– to love and care for everyone alive; that they might see their duty to men– to choose only the best, and then to bear and rear better ones; that they might see their duty as human beings, and come right out into full life and work and happiness!

I stopped, breathless, with shining eyes. I waited, trembling, for things to happen. Nothing happened.

You see, this magic which had fallen on me was black magic– and I had wished white. It didn't work at all, and, what was worse, it stopped all the other things that were working so nicely.

Oh, if I had only thought to wish permanence for those lovely punishments! If only I had done more while I could do it, had half appreciated my privileges when I was a Witch!

* * * * *

A Middle-Sized Artist

When Rosamond's brown eyes seemed almost too big for her brilliant little face, and her brown curls danced on her shoulders, she had a passionate enthusiasm for picture books. She loved "the reading," but when the picture made what her young mind was trying to grasp suddenly real before her, the stimulus reaching the brain from two directions at once, she used to laugh with delight and hug the book.

The vague new words describing things she never saw suggested "castle," a thing of gloom and beauty; and then upon the page came The Castle itself, looming dim and huge before her, with drooping heavy banners against the sunset calm.

How she had regretted it, scarce knowing why, when the pictures were less real than the description; when the princess, whose beauty made her the Rose of the World (her name was Rosamond, too!), appeared in visible form no prettier, no, not as pretty, as The Fair One with The Golden Locks in the other book! And what an outcry she made to her indifferent family when first confronted by the unbelievable blasphemy of an illustration that differed from the text!

"But, Mother— see!" she cried. "It says, 'Her beauty was crowned by rich braids of golden hair, wound thrice around her shapely head,' and this girl has black hair— in curls! Did the man forget what he just said?" Her mother didn't seem to care at all. "They often get them wrong," she said. "Perhaps it was an old plate. Run away, dear, Mama is very busy."

But Rosamond cared. She asked her father more particularly about this mysterious "old plate," and he, being a publisher, was able to give her more information. She learned that these wonderful reinforcements of her adored stories did not emanate direct from the brain of the beneficent author, but were a supplementary product by some draughtsman, who cared far less for what was in the author's mind than for what was in his own; who was sometimes lazy, sometimes arrogant, sometimes incompetent; sometimes all three. That to find a real artist, who could make pictures and was willing to make them like the picture the author saw, was very unusual.

"You see, little girl," said Papa, "the big artists are too big to do it— they'd rather make their own pictures; and the little artists are too little— they can't make real ones of their own ideas, nor yet of another's."

"Aren't there any middle-sized artists?" asked the child.

"Sometimes," said her father; and then he showed her some of the perfect illustrations which leave nothing to be desired, as the familiar ones by Teniel and Henry Holiday, which make Alice's Adventures and the Hunting of the Snark so doubly dear, Dore and Retsch and Tony Johannot and others.

"When I grow up," said Rosamond decidedly, "I'm going to be a middle-sized artist!" Fortunately for her aspirations the line of study required was in no way different at first from that of general education. Her parents explained that a good illustrator ought to know pretty much everything. So she obediently went through school and college, and when the time came for real work at her drawing there was no objection to that.

"It is pretty work," said her mother, "a beautiful accomplishment. It will always be a resource for her."

"A girl is better off to have an interest," said her father, "and not marry the first fool that asks her. When she does fall in love this won't stand in the way; it never does; with a woman. Besides — she may need it sometime."

So her father helped and her mother did not hinder, and when the brown eyes were less disproportionate and the brown curls wreathed high upon her small fine head, she found herself at twenty-one more determined to be a middle-sized artist than she was at ten.

Then love came; in the person of one of her father's readers; a strenuous new-fledged college graduate; big, handsome, domineering, opinionated; who was accepting a salary of four dollars a week for the privilege of working in a publishing house, because he loved books and meant to write them some day.

They saw a good deal of each other, and were pleasantly congenial. She sympathized with his criticisms of modem fiction; he sympathized with her criticisms of modern illustration; and her young imagination began to stir with sweet memories of poetry and romance; and sweet hopes of beautiful reality.

There are cases where the longest way round is the shortest way home; but Mr. Allen G. Goddard chose differently. He had read much about women and about love, beginning with a full foundation from the ancients; but lacked an understanding of the modern woman, such as he had to deal with.

Therefore, finding her evidently favorable, his theories and inclinations suiting, he made hot love to her, breathing, "My Wife!" into her ear before she had scarce dared to think "my darling!" and suddenly wrapping her in his arms with hot kisses, while she was still musing on "The Huguenot Lovers" and the kisses she dared dream of came in slow gradation as in the Sonnets From the Portuguese.

He was in desperate earnest. "O you are so beautiful!" he cried. "So unbelievably beautiful! Come to me, my Sweet!" for she had sprung away and stood panting and looking at him, half reproachful, half angry.

"You love me, Dearest! You cannot deny it!" he cried. "And I love you— Ah! You shall know!"

He was single-hearted, sincere; stirred by a very genuine overwhelming emotion. She on the contrary was moved by many emotions at once;— a pleasure she was half ashamed of; a disappointment she could not clearly define; as if some one had told her the whole plot of a promising new novel; a sense of fear of the new hopes she had been holding, and of startled loyalty to her long-held purposes.

"Stop!" she said— for he evidently mistook her agitation, and thought her silence was consent. "I suppose I do— love you— a little; but you've no right to kiss me like that!"

His eyes shone. "You Darling! My Darling!" he said. "You will give me the right, won't you? Now, Dearest— see! I am waiting!" And he held out his arms to her.

But Rosamond was more and more displeased. "You will have to wait. I'm sorry; but I'm not ready to be engaged, yet! You know my plans. Why I'm going to Paris this year! I'm going to work! It will be ever so long before I'm ready to— to settle down."

"As to that," he said more calmly, "I cannot of course offer immediate marriage, but we can wait for that— together! You surely will not leave me— if you love me!"

"I think I love you," she said conscientiously, "at least I did think so. You've upset it all, somehow— you hurry me so!— no— I can't bind myself yet."

"Do you tell me to wait for you?" he asked; his deep voice still strong to touch her heart. "How long, Dearest?"

"I'm not asking you to wait for me— I don't want to promise anything— nor to have you. But when I have made a place— am really doing something— perhaps then—"

He laughed harshly. "Do not deceive yourself, child, nor me! If you loved me there would be none of this poor wish for freedom— for a career. You don't love me— that's all!"

He waited for her to deny this. She said nothing. He did not know how hard it was for her to keep from crying— and from running to his arms.

"Very well," said he. "Goodbye!"— And he was gone.

All that happened three years ago. Allen Goddard took it very hard; and added to his earlier ideas about women another, that "the new woman" was a selfish heartless creature, indifferent to her own true nature. He had to stay where he was and work, owing to the pressure of circumstances, which made it harder; so he became something of a misogynist; which is not a bad thing when a young man has to live on very little and build a place for himself.

In spite of this cynicism he could not remove from his mind those softly brilliant dark eyes; the earnest thoughtful lines of the pure young face; and the changing lights and shadows in that silky hair. Also, in the course of his work, he was continually reminded of her; for her characteristic drawings appeared more and frequently in the magazines, and grew better, stronger, more convincing from year to year.

Stories of adventure she illustrated admirably; children's stories to perfection; fairy stories— she was the delight of thousands of children, who never once thought that the tiny quaint rose in a circle that was to be found in all those charming pictures meant a name. But he noticed that she never illustrated love stories; and smiled bitterly, to himself.

And Rosamond? There were moments when she was inclined to forfeit her passage money and throw herself unreservedly into those strong arms which had held her so tightly for a little while. But a bud picked open does not bloom naturally; and her tumultuous feelings were thoroughly dissipated by a long strong attack of *mal de mer.*

She derived two advantages from her experience: one a period of safe indifference to all advances from eager fellow students and more cautious older admirers; the other a facility she had not before aspired to in the making of pictures of love and lovers. She made pictures of him from memory— so good, so moving, that she put them religiously away in a portfolio by themselves; and only took them out— sometimes. She illustrated, solely for her own enjoyment some of her girlhood's best loved poems and stories. "The Rhyme of the Duchess May," "The Letter L," "In a Balcony," "In a Gondola." And hid them from herself even— they rather frightened her.

After three years of work abroad she came home with an established reputation, plenty of orders, and an interest that would not be stifled in the present state of mind of Mr. Allen Goddard. She found him still at work, promoted to fifteen dollars a week by this time, and adding to his income by writing political and statistical articles for the magazines. He talked, when they met, of this work, with little enthusiasm, and asked her politely about hers.

"Anybody can see mine!" she told him lightly. "And judge it easily."

"Mine too," he answered. "It today is— and tomorrow is cast into the waste-basket. He who runs may read— if he runs fast enough."

He told himself he was glad he was not bound to this hard, bright creature, so unnaturally self-sufficient, and successful. She told herself that he had never cared for her, really, that was evident.

Then an English publisher who liked her work sent her a new novel by a new writer, "A. Gage." "I know this is out of your usual line," he said, "but I want a woman to do it, and I want you to be the woman, if possible. Read it and see what you think. Any terms you like."

The novel was called "Two and One;" and she began it with languid interest, because she liked that publisher and wished to give full reasons for refusing. It opened with two young people who were much in love with one another; the girl a talented young sculptor with a vivid desire for fame; and another girl, a cousin of the man, ordinary enough, but pretty and sweet, and with no desires save those of romance and domesticity. The first couple broke off a happy engagement because she insisted on studying in Paris, and her lover, who could neither go with her, nor immediately marry her, naturally objected.

Rosamond sat up in bed; pulled a shawl round her, swung the electric light nearer, and went on. The man was broken-hearted; he suffered tortures of loneliness, disappointment, doubt, self-depreciation. He waited, held at his work by a dependent widowed mother; hoping against hope that his lost one would come back.

The girl meanwhile made good in her art work; she was not a great sculptor but a popular portraitist and maker of little genre groups. She had other offers, but refused them, being hardened in her ambitions, and, possibly, still withheld by her early love.

The man after two or three years of empty misery and hard grinding work, falls desperately ill; the pretty cousin helps the mother nurse him, and shows her own affection. He offers the broken remnants of his heart, which she eagerly undertakes to patch up; and they become tolerably happy, at least she is.

But the young sculptor in Paris! Rosamond hurried through the pages to the last chapter. There was the haughty and triumphant heroine in her studio. She had been given a medal— she had plenty of orders— she had just refused a Count. Everyone had gone, and she sat alone in her fine studio, self-satisfied and triumphant.

Then she picks up an old American paper which was lying about; reads it idly as she smokes her cigarette— and then both paper and cigarette drop to the floor, and she sits staring.

Then she starts up— her arms out— vainly. "Wait! O Wait!" she cries—" I was coming back,"— and drops into her chair again. The fire is out. She is alone.

Rosamond shut the book and leaned back upon her pillow. Her eyes were shut tight; but a little gleaming line showed on either cheek under the near light. She put the light out and lay quite still.

Allen G. Goddard, in his capacity as "reader" was looking over some popular English novels which his firm wished to arrange about publishing in America. He left "Two and One" to the last. It was the second edition, the illustrated one which he had not seen yet; the first he had read before. He regarded it from time to time with a peculiar expression.

"Well," he said to himself, "I suppose I can stand it if the others do." And he opened the book.

The drawing was strong work certainly, in a style he did not know. They were striking pictures, vivid, real, carrying out in last detail the descriptions given, and the very spirit of the book, showing it more perfectly than the words. There was the tender happiness of the lovers, the courage, the firmness, the fixed purpose in the young sculptor insisting on her freedom, and the joyful pride of the successful artist in her work.

There was beauty and charm in this character, yet the face was always turned away, and there was a haunting suggestion of familiarity in the figure.

The other girl was beautiful, and docile in expression; well-dressed and graceful; yet somehow unattractive, even at her best, as nurse; and the man was extremely well drawn, both in his happy ardor as a lover, and his grinding misery when rejected. He was very good-looking; and here too was this strong sense of resemblance.

"Why he looks like me!" suddenly cried the reader— springing to his feet. "Confound his impudence!" he cried. "How in thunder!"

Then he looked at the picture again, more carefully, a growing suspicion in his face; and turned hurriedly to the title page,— seeing a name unknown to him. This subtle, powerful convincing work; this man who undeniably suggested him; this girl whose eyes he could not see; he turned from one to another and hurried to the back of the book.

"The fire was out— she was alone." And there, in the remorseless light of a big lamp before her fireless hearth, the crumpled newspaper beside her, and all hope gone from a limp, crouching little figure, sat— why, he would know her among a thousand— even if her face was buried in her hands, and sunk on the arm of the chair— it was Rosamond!

She was in her little downtown room and hard at work when he entered; but she had time to conceal a new book quickly. He came straight to her; he had a book in his hand, open— he held it out.

"Did you do this?" he demanded. "Tell me— tell me!" His voice was very unreliable. She lifted her eyes slowly to his; large, soft, full of dancing lights, and the rich color swept to the gold-lighted borders of her hair.

"Did you?" she asked.

He was taken aback. "I!" said he. "Why it's by—" he showed her the title-page. "By A. Gage," he read.

"Yes," said she, "Go on," and he went on, 'Illustrated by A. N. Other.'"

"It's a splendid novel," she said seriously. "Real work— great work. I always knew you'd do it, Allen. I'm so proud of you!" And she held out her hand in the sincere intelligent appreciation of a fellow craftsman. He took it, still bewildered.

"Thank you," he said. "I value your opinion— honestly I do! And— with a sudden sweep of recognition. "And yours is great work! Superb! Why you've put more into that story than I knew was there! You make the thing live and breathe!

You've put a shadow of remorse in that lonely ruffian there that I was too proud to admit! And you've shown the— unconvincingness of that Other Girl; marvelously. But see here— no more fooling!"

He took her face between his hands, hands that quivered

strongly, and forced her to look at him. "Tell me about that last picture! Is it— true?"

Her eyes met his, with the look he longed for. "It is true," she said.

After some time, really it was a long time, but they had not noticed it, he suddenly burst forth. "But how did you know?"

She lifted a flushed and smiling face: and pointed to the title page again.

"'A. Gage.'— You threw it down."

"And you—" He threw back his head and laughed delightedly. "You threw down A-N-Other! O you witch! You immeasurably clever darling! How well our work fits. By Jove! What good times we'll have!"

And they did.

* * * * *

Turned

In her soft-carpeted, thick-curtained, richly furnished chamber, Mrs Marroner lay sobbing on the wide, soft bed. She sobbed bitterly, chokingly, despairingly; her shoulders heaved and shook convulsively; her hands were tight-clenched.

She had forgotten her elaborate dress, the more elaborate bed-cover; forgotten her dignity, her self-control, her pride. In her mind was an overwhelming, unbelievable horror, an immeasurable loss, a turbulent, struggling mass of emotion. In her reserved, superior, Boston-bred life, she had never dreamed that it would be possible for her to feel so many things at once, and with such trampling intensity.

She tried to cool her feelings into thoughts; to stiffen them into words; to control herself— and could not. It brought vaguely to her mind an awful moment in the breakers at York Beach, one summer in girlhood when she had been swimming under water and could not find the top.

In her uncarpeted, thin-curtained, poorly furnished chamber on the top floor, Gerta Petersen lay sobbing on the narrow, hard bed. She was of larger frame than her mistress, grandly built and strong; but all her proud young womanhood was prostrate now, convulsed with agony, dissolved in tears. She did not try to control herself. She wept for two.

If Mrs Marroner suffered more from the wreck and ruin of a longer love— perhaps a deeper one; if her tastes were finer, her ideals loftier; if she bore the pangs of bitter jealousy and outraged pride, Gerta had personal shame to meet, a hopeless future, and a looming present which filled her with unreasoning terror.

She had come like a meek young goddess into that perfectly ordered house, strong, beautiful, full of goodwill and eager obedience, but ignorant and childish— a girl of eighteen.

Mr Marroner had frankly admired her, and so had his wife. They discussed her visible perfections and her visible limitations with that perfect confidence which they had so long enjoyed. Mrs Marroner was not a jealous woman. She had never been jealous in her life— till now.

Gerta had stayed and learned their ways. They had both been fond of her. Even the cook was fond of her. She was what is called 'willing', was unusually teachable and plastic; and Mrs Marroner, with her early habits of giving instruction, tried to educate her somewhat.

'I never saw anyone so docile,' Mrs Marroner had often commented. 'It is perfection in a servant, but almost a defect in character. She is helpless and confiding.'

She was precisely that: a tall, rosy-cheeked baby; rich womanhood without, helpless infancy within. Her braided wealth of dead-gold hair, her grave blue eyes, her mighty shoulders and long, firmly molded limbs seemed those of a primal earth spirit; but she was only an ignorant child, with a child's weakness.

When Mr Marroner had to go abroad for his firm, unwillingly, hating to leave his wife, he had told her he felt quite safe to leave her in Gerta's hands— she would take care of her.

'Be good to your mistress, Gerta,' he told the girl that last morning at breakfast. 'I leave her to you to take care of. I shall be back in a month at latest.' Then he turned, smiling, to his wife. 'And you must take care of Gerta, too,' he said. 'I expect you'll have her ready for college when I get back.'

This was seven months ago. Business had delayed him from week to week, from month to month. He wrote to his wife, long, loving, frequent letters, deeply regretting the delay, explaining how necessary, how profitable it was, congratulating her on the wide resources she had, her well-filled, well-balanced mind, her many interests.

'If I should be eliminated from your scheme of things, by any of those "acts of God" mentioned on the tickets, I do not feel that you would be an utter wreck,' he said. 'That is very comforting to me. Your life is so rich and wide that no one loss, even a great one, would wholly cripple you. But nothing of the sort is likely to happen, and I shall be home again in three weeks— if this thing gets settled. And you will be looking so lovely, with that eager light in your eyes and the changing flush I know so well— and love so well! My dear wife! We shall have to have a new honeymoon— other moons come every month, why shouldn't the mellifluous kind?'

He often asked after 'little Gerta', sometimes enclosed a picture postcard to her, joked his wife about her laborious efforts to educate 'the child', was so loving and merry and wise—

All this was racing through Mrs Marroner's mind as she lay there with the broad, hemstitched border of fine linen sheeting crushed and twisted in one hand, and the other holding a sodden handkerchief.

She had tried to teach Gerta, and had grown to love the patient, sweet-natured child, in spite of her dullness. At work with her hands, she was clever, if not quick, and could keep small accounts from week to week. But to the woman who held a Ph.D., who had been on the faculty of a college, it was like baby-tending. Perhaps having no babies of her own made her love the big child the more, though the years between them were but fifteen.

To the girl she seemed quite old, of course; and her young heart was full of grateful affection for the patient care which made her feel so much at home in this new land. And then she had noticed a shadow on the girl's bright face. She looked nervous, anxious, worried. When the bell rang, she seemed startled, and would rush hurriedly to the door. Her peals of frank laughter no longer rose from the area gate as she stood talking with the always admiring tradesmen.

Mrs Marroner had labored long to teach her more reserve with men, and flattered herself that her words were at last effective. She suspected the girl of homesickness, which was denied. She suspected her of illness, which was denied also. At last she suspected her of something which could not be denied.

For a long time she refused to believe it, waiting. Then she had to believe it, but schooled herself to patience and understanding. 'The poor child,' she said. 'She is here without a mother— she is so foolish and yielding— I must not be too stern with her.' And she tried to win the girl's confidence with wise, kind words. But Gerta had literally thrown herself at her feet and begged her with streaming tears not to turn her away. She would admit nothing, explain nothing, but frantically promised to work for Mrs Marroner as long as she lived— if only she would keep her.

Revolving the problem carefully in her mind, Mrs Marroner thought she would keep her, at least for the present. She tried to repress her sense of ingratitude in one she had so sincerely tried to help, and the cold, contemptuous anger she had always felt for such weakness.

'The thing to do now,' she said to herself, 'is to see her through this safely. The child's life should not be hurt any more than is unavoidable. I will ask Dr Bleet about it—what a comfort a woman doctor is! I'll stand by the poor, foolish thing till it's over, and then get her back to Sweden somehow with her baby. How they do come where they are not wanted— and don't come where they are wanted!'

Mrs Marroner, sitting alone in the quiet, spacious beauty of the house, almost envied Gerta. Then came the deluge. She had sent the girl out for needed air toward dark. The late mail came; she took it in herself. One letter for her— her husband's letter. She knew the postmark, the stamp, the kind of typewriting. She impulsively kissed it in the dim hall. No one would suspect Mrs Marroner of kissing her husband's letters— but she did, often.

She looked over the others. One was for Gerta, and not from Sweden. It looked precisely like her own. This struck her as a little odd, but Mr Marroner had several times sent messages and cards to the girl. She laid the letter on the hall table and took hers to her room.

'My poor child,' it began. What letter of hers had been sad enough to warrant that? 'I am deeply concerned at the news you send.' What news to so concern him had she written? 'You must bear it bravely, little girl. I shall be home soon, and will take care of you, of course. I hope there is not immediate anxiety— you do not say. Here is money, in case you need it. I expect to get home in a month at best. If you have to go, be sure to leave your address at my office. Cheer up— be brave— I will take care of you.'

The letter was typewritten, which was not unusual. It was unsigned, which was unusual. It enclosed an American bill— fifty dollars. It did not seem in the least like any letter she had ever had from her husband, or any letter she could imagine him writing. But a strange, cold feeling was creeping over her, like a flood rising around a house. She utterly refused to admit the ideas which began to bob and push about outside her mind, and to force themselves in. Yet under the pressure of these repudiated thoughts she went downstairs and brought up the other letter— the letter to Gerta.

She laid them side by side on a smooth dark space on the table; marched to the piano and played, with stern precision, refusing to think, till the girl came back. When she came in, Mrs Marroner rose quietly and came to the table. 'Here is a letter for you,' she said.

The girl stepped forward eagerly, saw the two lying together there, hesitated, and looked at her mistress.

'Take yours, Gerta. Open it, please.'

The girl turned frightened eyes upon her.

'I want you to read it, here,' said Mrs Marroner.

'Oh, ma'am—No! Please don't make me!'

'Why not?'

There seemed to be no reason at hand, and Gerta flushed more deeply and opened her letter. It was long; it was evidently puzzling to her; it began 'My dear wife.' She read it slowly.

'Are you sure it is your letter?' asked Mrs Marroner. 'Is not this one yours? Is not that one— mine?'

She held out the other letter to her.

'It is a mistake,' Mrs Marroner went on, with a hard quietness. She had lost her social bearings somehow, lost her usual keen sense of the proper thing to do. This was not life; this was a nightmare.

'Do you not see? Your letter was put in my envelope and my letter was put in your envelope. Now we understand it.'

But poor Gerta had no antechamber to her mind, no trained forces to preserve order while agony entered. The thing swept over her, resistless, overwhelming. She cowered before the outraged wrath she expected; and from some hidden cavern that wrath arose and swept over her in pale flame.

'Go and pack your trunk,' said Mrs Marroner. 'You will leave my house tonight. Here is your money.' She laid down the fifty-dollar bill. She put with it a month's wages. She had no shadow of pity for those anguished eyes, those tears which she heard drop on the floor.

'Go to your room and pack,' said Mrs Marroner. And Gerta, always obedient, went. Then Mrs Marroner went to hers, and spent a time she never counted, lying on her face on the bed. But the training of the twenty-eight years which had elapsed before her marriage; the life at college, both as student and teacher; the independent growth which she had made, formed a very different background for grief from that in Gerta's mind.

After a while Mrs Marroner arose. She administered to herself a hot bath, a cold shower, a vigorous rubbing. 'Now I can think,' she said. First she regretted the sentence of instant banishment. She went upstairs to see if it had been carried out. Poor Gerta! The tempest of her agony had worked itself out at last as in a child, and left her sleeping, the pillow wet, the lips still grieving, a big sob shuddering itself off now and then.

Mrs Marroner stood and watched her, and as she watched she considered the helpless sweetness of the face; the defenseless, unformed character; the docility and habit of obedience which made her so attractive— and so easily a victim. Also she thought of the mighty force which had swept over her; of the great process now working itself out through her; of how pitiful and futile seemed any resistance she might have made.

She softly returned to her own room, made up a little fire, and sat by it, ignoring her feelings now, as she had before ignored her thoughts.

Here were two women and a man. One woman was a wife: loving, trusting, affectionate. One was a servant: loving, trusting, affectionate— a young girl, an exile, a dependent; grateful for any kindness; untrained, uneducated, childish. She ought, of course, to have resisted temptation; but Mrs Marroner was wise enough to know how difficult temptation is to recognize when it comes in the guise of friendship and from a source one does not suspect.

Gerta might have done better in resisting the grocer's clerk; had, indeed, with Mrs Marroner's advice, resisted several. But where respect was due, how could she criticize? Where obedience was due, how could she refuse— with ignorance to hold her blinded— until too late?

As the older, wiser woman forced herself to understand and extenuate the girl's misdeed and foresee her ruined future, a new feeling rose in her heart, strong, clear, and overmastering: a sense of measureless condemnation for the man who had done this thing. He knew. He understood. He could fully foresee and measure the consequences of his act. He appreciated to the full the innocence, the ignorance, the grateful affection, the habitual docility, of which he deliberately took advantage.

Mrs Marroner rose to icy peaks of intellectual apprehension, from which her hours of frantic pain seemed far indeed removed. He had done this thing under the same roof with her— his wife. He had not frankly loved the younger woman, broken with his wife, made a new marriage. That would have been heart-break pure and simple. This was something else.

That letter, that wretched, cold, carefully guarded, unsigned letter, that bill— far safer than a check— these did not speak of affection. Some men can love two women at one time. This was not love.

Mrs Marroner's sense of pity and outrage for herself, the wife, now spread suddenly into a perception of pity and outrage for the girl. All that splendid, clean young beauty, the hope of a happy life, with marriage and motherhood, honorable independence, even— these were nothing to that man. For his own pleasure he had chosen to rob her of her life's best joys.

He would 'take care of her,' said the letter. How? In what capacity? And then, sweeping over both her feelings for herself, the wife, and Gerta, his victim, came a new flood, which literally lifted her to her feet. She rose and walked, her head held high.

'This is the sin of man against woman,' she said. 'The offense is against womanhood. Against motherhood. Against— the child.'

She stopped. The child. His child. That, too, he sacrificed and injured— doomed to degradation.

Mrs Marroner came of stern New England stock. She was not a Calvinist, hardly even a Unitarian, but the iron of Calvinism was in her soul: of that grim faith which held that most people had to be damned 'for the glory of God.'

Generations of ancestors who both preached and practiced stood behind her; people whose lives had been sternly molded to their highest moments of religious conviction. In sweeping bursts of feeling, they achieved 'conviction', and afterward they lived and died according to that conviction.

When Mr Marroner reached home a few weeks later, following his letters too soon to expect an answer to either, he saw no wife upon the pier, though he had cabled, and found the house closed darkly. He let himself in with his latch-key, and stole softly upstairs, to surprise his wife.

No wife was there. He rang the bell. No servant answered it. He turned up light after light, searched the house from top to bottom; it was utterly empty. The kitchen wore a clean, bald, unsympathetic aspect. He left it and slowly mounted the stairs, completely dazed. The whole house was clean, in perfect order, wholly vacant.

One thing he felt perfectly sure of— she knew. Yet was he sure? He must not assume too much. She might have been ill. She might have died. He started to his feet. No, they would have cabled him. He sat down again.

For any such change, if she had wanted him to know, she would have written. Perhaps she had, and he, returning so suddenly, had missed the letter. The thought was some comfort. It must be so. He turned to the telephone and again hesitated. If she had found out— if she had gone— utterly gone, without a word— should he announce it himself to friends and family?

He walked the floor; he searched everywhere for some letter, some word of explanation. Again and again he went to the telephone— and always stopped. He could not bear to ask: 'Do you know where my wife is?'

The harmonious, beautiful rooms reminded him in a dumb, helpless way of her— like the remote smile on the face of the dead. He put out the lights, could not bear the darkness, turned them all on again.

It was a long night—

In the morning he went early to the office. In the accumulated mail was no letter from her. No one seemed to know of anything unusual. A friend asked after his wife—' Pretty glad to see you, I guess?' He answered evasively.

About eleven, a man came to see him: John Hill, her lawyer. Her cousin, too. Mr Marroner had never liked him. He liked him less now, for Mr Hill merely handed him a letter, remarked, 'I was requested to deliver this to you personally,' and departed, looking like a person who is called on to kill something offensive.

'I have gone. I will care for Gerta. Goodbye. Marion.'

That was all. There was no date, no address, no postmark, nothing but that. In his anxiety and distress, he had fairly forgotten Gerta and all that. Her name aroused in him a sense of rage. She had come between him and his wife. She had taken his wife from him. That was the way he felt.

At first he said nothing, did nothing, lived on alone in his house, taking meals where he chose. When people asked him about his wife, he said she was traveling— for her health. He would not have it in the newspapers. Then, as time passed, as no enlightenment came to him, he resolved not to bear it any longer, and employed detectives. They blamed him for not having put them on the track earlier, but set to work, urged to the utmost secrecy.

What to him had been so blank a wall of mystery seemed not to embarrass them in the least. They made careful inquiries as to her 'past', found where she had studied, where taught, and on what lines; that she had some little money of her own, that her doctor was Josephine L. Bleet, M.D., and many other bits of information. As a result of careful and prolonged work, they finally told him that she had resumed teaching under one of her old professors, lived quietly, and apparently kept boarders; giving him town, street, and number, as if it were a matter of no difficulty whatever.

He had returned in early spring. It was autumn before he found her. A quiet college town in the hills, a broad, shady street, a pleasant house standing in its own lawn, with trees and flowers about it. He had the address in his hand, and the number showed clear on the white gate. He walked up the straight gravel path and rang the bell. An elderly servant opened the door.

'Does Mrs Marroner live here?'

'No, sir.'

'This is number twenty-eight?'

'Yes, sir.'

'Who does live here?'

'Miss Wheeling, sir.'

Ah! Her maiden name. They had told him, but he had forgotten. He stepped inside. 'I would like to see her,' he said.

He was ushered into a still parlor, cool and sweet with the scent of flowers, the flowers she had always loved best. It almost brought tears to his eyes.

All their years of happiness rose in his mind again— the exquisite beginnings; the days of eager longing before she was really his; the deep, still beauty of her love. Surely she would forgive him— she must forgive him. He would humble himself; he would tell her of his honest remorse— his absolute determination to be a different man.

Through the wide doorway there came in to him two women. One like a tall Madonna, bearing a baby in her arms.

Marion, calm, steady, definitely impersonal, nothing but a clear pallor to hint of inner stress.

Greta, holding the child as a bulwark, with a new intelligence in her face, and her blue, adoring eyes fixed on her friend— not upon him.

He looked from one to the other dumbly.

And the woman who had been his wife asked quietly:

'What have you to say to us?'

* * * * *

Charlotte Gilman

Her Housekeeper

On the top floor of a New York boarding-house lived a particularly attractive woman who was an actress. She was also a widow, not divorcee, but just plain widow; and she persisted in acting under her real name, which was Mrs. Leland. The manager objected, but her reputation was good enough to carry the point.

"It will cost you a great deal of money, Mrs. Leland," said the manager.

"I make money enough," she answered.

"You will not attract so many— admirers," said the manager.

"I have admirers enough," she answered; which was visibly true. She was well under thirty, even by daylight— and about eighteen on the stage; and as for admirers— they apparently thought Mrs. Leland was a carefully selected stage name.

Besides being a widow, she was a mother, having a small boy of about five years; and this small boy did not look in the least like a "stage child," but was a brown-skinned, healthy little rascal of the ordinary sort. With this boy, an excellent nursery governess, and a maid, Mrs. Leland occupied the top floor above mentioned, and enjoyed it. She had a big room in front, to receive in; and a small room with a skylight, to sleep in.

The boy's room and the governess' rooms were at the back, with sunny south windows, and the maid slept on a couch in the parlor. She was a colored lady, named Alice, and did not seem to care where she slept, or if she slept at all.

"I never was so comfortable in my life," said Mrs. Leland to her friends. "I've been here three years and mean to stay. It is not like any boarding-house I ever saw, and it is not like any home I ever had. I have the privacy, the detachment, the carelessness of a boarding-house, and all the comforts of a home. Up I go to my little top flat as private as you like. My Alice takes care of it—the housemaids only come in when I'm out. I can eat with the others downstairs if I please; but mostly I don't please; and up come my little meals on the dumbwaiter— hot and good."

"But— having to flock with a lot of promiscuous boarders!" said her friends.

"I don't flock, you see; that's just it. And besides, they are not promiscuous— there isn't a person in the house now who isn't some sort of a friend of mine. As fast as a room was vacated I'd suggest somebody— and here we all are. It's great."

"But do you like a skylight room?" Mrs. Leland's friends further inquired of her?"

"By no means!" she promptly replied. "I hate it. I feel like a mouse in a pitcher!"

"Then why in the name of reason—?"

"Because I can sleep there! Sleep!— It's the only way to be quiet in New York, and I have to sleep late if I sleep at all. I've fixed the skylight so that I'm drenched with air— and not drenched with rain!— and there I am. Johnny is gagged and muffled as it were, and carried downstairs as early as possible. He gets his breakfast, and the unfortunate Miss Merton has to go out and play with him— in all weathers— except kindergarten time. Then Alice sits on the stairs and keeps everybody away till I ring."

Possibly it was owing to the stillness and the air and the sleep till near lunchtime that Mrs. Leland kept her engaging youth, her vivid uncertain beauty. At times you said of her, "She has a keen intelligent face, but she's not pretty." Which was true. She was not pretty. But at times again she overcame you with her sudden loveliness. All of which was observed by her friend from the second floor who wanted to marry her. In this he was not alone; either as a friend, of whom she had many, or as a lover, of whom she had more. His distinction lay first in his opportunities, as a co-resident, for which he was heartily hated by all the more and some of the many; and second in that he remained a friend in spite of being a lover, and remained a lover in spite of being flatly refused.

His name in the telephone book was given "Arthur Olmstead, real estate;" office this and residence that— she looked him up there after their first meeting. He was rather a short man, heavily built, with a quiet kind face, and a somewhat quizzical smile. He seemed to make all the money he needed, occupied the two rooms and plentiful closet space of his floor in great contentment, and manifested most improper domesticity of taste by inviting friends to tea. "Just like a woman!" Mrs. Leland told him.

"And why not? Women have so many attractive ways— why not imitate them?" he asked her. "A man doesn't want to be feminine, I'm sure," struck in a pallid, overdressed youth, with openwork socks on his slim feet, and perfumed handkerchief.

Mr. Olmstead smiled a broad friendly smile. He was standing near the young man, a little behind him, and at this point he put his hands just beneath the youth's arms, lifted and set him aside as if he were an umbrella-stand. "Excuse me, Mr. Masters," he said gravely, but you were standing on Mrs. Leland's gown."

Mr. Masters was too much absorbed in apologizing to the lady to take umbrage at the method of his removal; but she was not so oblivious. She tried doing it to her little boy afterwards, and found him very heavy.

When she came home from her walk or drive in the early winter dusk, this large quietly furnished room, the glowing fire, the excellent tea and delicate thin bread and butter were most restful. "It is two more stories up before I can get my own;" she would say— "I must stop a minute."

When he began to propose to her the first time she tried to stop him. "O please don't!" she cried. "Please don't! There are no end of reasons why I will not marry anybody again. Why can't some of you men be nice to me and not— that! Now I can't come in to tea any more!"

"I'd like to know why not," said he calmly. "You don't have to marry me if you don't want to; but that's no reason for cutting my acquaintance, is it?"

She gazed at him in amazement.

"I'm not threatening to kill myself, am I? I don't intend going to the devil. I'd like to be your husband, but if I can't— may I not be a brother to you?"

She was inclined to think he was making fun of her, but no— his proposal had the real ring in it.

"And you're not— you're not going to—?" it seemed the baldest assumption to think that he was going to, he looked so strong and calm and friendly.

"Not going to annoy you? Not going to force an undesired affection on you and rob myself of a most agreeable friendship? Of course not. Your tea is cold, Mrs. Leland— let me give you another cup. And do you think Miss Rose is going to do well as 'Angelina?'"

So Mrs. Leland was quite relieved in her mind, and free to enjoy the exceeding comfortableness of this relation.

Little Johnny was extremely fond of Mr Olmstead; who always treated him with respect, and who could listen to his tales of strife and glory more intelligently than either mother or governess.

Mr. Olmstead kept on hand a changing supply of interesting things; not toys— never, but real things not intended for little boys to play with. No little boy would want to play with dolls for instance; but what little boy would not be fascinated by a small wooden lay figure, capable of unheard-of contortions.

Tin soldiers were common, but the flags of all nations— real flags, and true stories about them, were interesting. Noah's arks were cheap and unreliable scientifically; but Barye lions, ivory elephants, and Japanese monkeys in didactic groups of three, had unfailing attraction. And the books this man had— great solid books that could be opened wide on the floor, and a little boy lie down to in peace and comfort!

Mrs. Leland stirred her tea and watched them until Johnny was taken upstairs. "Why don't you smoke?" she asked suddenly. "Doctor's orders?"

"No— mine," he answered. "I never consulted a doctor in my life."

"Nor a dentist, I judge," said she.

"Nor a dentist."

"You'd better knock on wood!" she told him.

"And cry 'Uncle Reuben?' he asked smilingly.

"You haven't told me why you don't smoke!" said she suddenly.

"Haven't I?" he said. "That was very rude of me. But look here. There's a thing I wanted to ask you. Now I'm not pressing any sort of inquiry as to myself; but as a brother, would you mind telling me some of those numerous reasons why you will not marry anybody?"

She eyed him suspiciously, but he was as solid and calm as usual, regarding her pleasantly and with no hint of ulterior purpose.

"Why— I don't mind," she began slowly. "First— I have been married— and was very unhappy. That's reason enough."

He did not contradict her; but merely said, "That's one," and set it down in his notebook.

"Dear me, Mr. Olmstead! You're not a reporter, are you!"

"O no— but I wanted to have them clear and think about them," he explained. "Do you mind?" And he made as if to shut his little book again.

"I don't know as I mind," she said slowly. "But it looks so— businesslike."

"This is a very serious business, Mrs. Leland, as you must know. Quite aside from any personal desire of my own, I am truly 'your sincere friend and well-wisher,' as the Complete Letter Writer has it, and there are so many men wanting to marry you."

This she knew full well, and gazed pensively at the toe of her small flexible slipper, poised on a stool before the fire. Olmstead also gazed at the slipper toe with appreciation.

"What's the next one?" he said cheerfully.

"Do you know you are a real comfort," she told him suddenly. "I never knew a man before who could— well leave off being a man for a moment and just be a human creature."

"Thank you, Mrs. Leland," he said in tones of pleasant sincerity. "I want to be a comfort to you if I can. Incidentally wouldn't you be more comfortable on this side of the fire— the light falls better— don't move." And before she realized what he was doing he picked her up, chair and all, and put her down softly on the other side, setting the footstool as before, and even daring to place her little feet upon it— but with so businesslike an air that she saw no opening for rebuke. It is a difficult matter to object to a man's doing things like that when he doesn't look as if he was doing them.

"That's better," said he cheerfully, taking the place where she had been. "Now, what's the next one?"

"The next one is my boy."

"Second— Boy," he said, putting it down. "But I should think he'd be a reason the other way. Excuse me— I wasn't going to criticize— yet! And the third?"

"Why should you criticize at all, Mr. Olmstead?"

"I shouldn't— on my own account. But there may come a man you love."

He had a fine baritone voice. When she heard him sing Mrs. Leland always wished he were taller, handsomer, more distinguished looking; his voice sounded as if he were. "And I should hate to see these reasons standing in the way of your happiness," he continued.

"Perhaps they wouldn't," said she in a revery.

"Perhaps they wouldn't— and in that case it is no possible harm that you tell me the rest of them. I won't cast it up at you. Third?"

"Third, I won't give up my profession for any man alive."

"Any man alive would be a fool to want you to," said he setting down, "Third—Profession."

"Fourth— I like Freedom!" she said with sudden intensity. "You don't know!— they kept me so tight!— so tight— when I was a girl! Then— I was left alone, with very little money, and I began to study for the stage— that was like heaven! And then— O what idiots women are!" She said the word not tragically, but with such hard-pointed intensity that it sounded like a gimlet.

"Then I married, you see— I gave up all my new-won freedom to marry!— and he kept me tighter than ever."

She shut her expressive mouth in level lines— stood up suddenly and stretched her arms wide and high. "I'm free again, free— I can do exactly as I please!" The words were individually relished. "I have the work I love. I can earn all I need— am saving something for the boy. I'm perfectly independent!"

"And perfectly happy!" he cordially endorsed her. "I don't blame you for not wanting to give it up."

"O well— happy!" she hesitated. "There are times, of course, when one isn't happy. But then— the other way I was unhappy all the time."

"He's dead— unfortunately," mused Olmstead.

"Unfortunately?— Why?"

He looked at her with his straightforward, pleasant smile. "I'd have liked the pleasure of killing him," he said regretfully.

She was startled, and watched him with dawning alarm. But he was quite quiet— even cheerful. "Fourth— Freedom," he wrote. "Is that all?"

"No— there are two more. Neither of them will please you. You won't think so much of me any more. The worst one is this. I like — lovers! I'm very much ashamed of it, but I do! I try not to be unfair to them— some I really try to keep away from me— but honestly I like admiration and lots of it."

"What's the harm of that?" he asked easily, setting down, "Fifth— Lovers."

"No harm, so long as I'm my own mistress," said she defiantly. "I take care of my boy, I take care of myself— let them take care of themselves! Don't blame me too much!"

"You're not a very good psychologist, I'm afraid," said he.

"What do you mean?" she asked rather nervously.

"You surely don't expect a man to blame you for being a woman, do you?"

"All women are not like that," she hastily asserted. "They are too conscientious. Lots of my friends blame me severely."

"Women friends," he ventured.

"Men, too. Some men have said very hard things of me."

"Because you turned them down. That's natural."

"You don't!"

"No, I don't. I'm different.".

"How different?" she asked.

He looked at her steadily. His eyes were hazel, flecked with changing bits of color, deep, steady, with a sort of inner light that grew as she watched till she thought it well to consider her slipper again; and continued, "The sixth is as bad as the other almost. I hate— I'd like to write a dozen tragic plays to show how much I hate— Housekeeping! There! That's all!"

"Sixth— Housekeeping," he wrote down, quite unmoved. "But why should anyone blame you for that— it's not your business."

"No— thank goodness, it's not! And never will be! I'm free, I tell you and I stay free!— But look at the clock!" And she whisked away to dress for dinner.

He was not at table that night— not at home that night— not at home for some days— the landlady said he had gone out of town; and Mrs. Leland missed her afternoon tea. She had it upstairs, of course, and people came in— both friends and lovers; but she missed the quiet and coziness of the green and brown room downstairs.

Johnny missed his big friend still more. "Mama, where's Mr. Olmstead? Mama, why don't Mr. Olmstead come back? Mama! When is Mr. Olmstead coming back? Mama! Why don't you write to Mr. Olmstead and tell him to come back? Mama!— can't we go in there and play with his things?"

As if in answer to this last wish she got a little note from him saying simply, "Don't let Johnny miss the lions and monkeys— he and Miss Merton and you, of course, are quite welcome to the whole floor. Go in at any time."

Just to keep the child quiet she took advantage of this offer, and Johnnie introduced her to all the ins and outs of the place. In a corner of the bedroom was a zinc-lined tray with clay in it, where Johnnie played rapturously at making "making country." While he played his mother noted the quiet good taste and individuality of the place.

"It smells so clean!" she said to herself. "There! he hasn't told me yet why he doesn't smoke. I never told him I didn't like it."

Johnnie tugged at a bureau drawer. "He keeps the water in here!" he said, and before she could stop him he had out a little box with bits of looking-glass in it, which soon became lakes and rivers in his clay continent. Mrs. Leland put them back afterward, admiring the fine quality and goodly number of garments in that drawer, and their perfect order. Her husband had been a man who made a chowder of his bureau drawers, and who expected her to find all his studs and put them in for him.

"A man like this would be no trouble at all," she thought for a moment— but then she remembered other things and set her mouth hard. "Not for mine!" she said determinedly.

By and by he came back, serene as ever, friendly and unpresuming.

"Aren't you going to tell me why you don't smoke?" she suddenly demanded of him on another quiet dusky afternoon when tea was before them. He seemed so impersonal, almost remote, though nicer than ever to Johnny; and Mrs. Leland rather preferred the personal note in conservation.

"Why of course I am," he replied cordially. "That's easy," and he fumbled in his inner pocket.

"Is that where you keep your reasons?" she mischievously inquired.

"It's where I keep yours," he promptly answered, producing the little notebook.

"Now look here— I've got these all answered— you won't be able to hold to one of them after this. May I sit by you and explain?" She made room for him on the sofa amiably enough, but defied him to convince her. "Go ahead," she said cheerfully.

"First," he read off, "Previous Marriage. This is not a sufficient objection. Because you have been married you now know what to choose and what to avoid. A girl is comparatively helpless in this matter; you are armed. That your first marriage was unhappy is a reason for trying it again. It is not only that you are better able to choose, but that by the law of chances you stand to win next time. Do you admit the justice of this reasoning?"

"I don't admit anything," she said. "I'm waiting to ask you a question."

"Ask it now."

"No— I'll wait till you are all through. Do go on."

"'Second— The Boy,'" he continued. "Now Mrs. Leland, solely on the boy's account I should advise you to marry again. While he is a baby a mother is enough, but the older he grows the more he will need a father. Of course you should select a man the child could love— a man who could love the child."

"I begin to suspect you of deep double-dyed surreptitious designs, Mr. Olmstead. You know Johnnie loves you dearly. And you know I won't marry you," she hastily added.

"I'm not asking you to— now, Mrs. Leland. I did, in good faith, and I would again if I thought I had the shadow of a chance— but I'm not at present. Still, I'm quite willing to stand as an instance. Now, we might resume, on that basis. Objection one does not really hold against me— now does it?"

He looked at her cheerily, warmly, openly; and in his clean, solid strength and tactful kindness he was so unspeakably different from the dark, fascinating slender man who had become a nightmare to her youth, that she felt in her heart he was right— so far. "I won't admit a thing," she said sweetly. "But, pray go on."

He went on, unabashed. "'Second— Boy,' Now if you married me I should consider the boy as an added attraction. Indeed— if you do marry again— someone who doesn't want the boy— I wish you'd give him to me. I mean it. I think he loves me, and I think I could be of real service to the child." He seemed almost to have forgotten her, and she watched him curiously.

"Now, to go on," he continued. "'Third-Profession.' As to your profession," said he slowly, clasping his hands over one knee and gazing at the dark soft-colored rug, "if you married me, and gave up your profession I should find it a distinct loss, I should lose my favorite actress." She gave a little start of surprise.

"Didn't you know how much I admire your work?" he said. "I don't hang around the stage entrance— there are plenty of chappies to do that; and I don't always occupy a box and throw bouquets— I don't like a box anyhow. But I haven't missed seeing you in any part you've played yet— some of them I've seen a dozen times. And you're growing— you'll do better work still. It is sometimes a little weak in the love parts— seems as if you couldn't quite take it seriously— couldn't let yourself go— but you'll grow. You'll do better—I really think—after you're married "

She was rather impressed by this, but found it rather difficult to say anything; for he was not looking at her at all. He took up his notebook again with a smile. "So— if you married me, you would be more than welcome to go on with your profession. I wouldn't stand in your way any more than I do now.

'Fourth— Freedom,'" he read slowly. "That is easy in one way — hard in another. If you married me,"— She stirred resentfully at this constant reference to their marriage; but he seemed purely hypothetical in tone; "I wouldn't interfere with your freedom any. Not of my own will. But if you ever grew to love me— or if there were children— it would make some difference. Not much. There mightn't be any children, and it isn't likely you'd ever love me enough to have that stand in your way. Otherwise than that you'd have freedom— as much as now. A little more; because if you wanted to make a foreign tour, or anything like that, I'd take care of Johnnie. 'Fifth— Lovers.'" Here he paused leaning forward with his chin in his hands, his eyes bent down. She could see the broad heavy shoulders, the smooth fit of the well-made, coat, the spotless collar, and the fine, strong, clean-cut neck.

As it happened she particularly disliked the neck of the average man— either the cordy, the beefy or the adipose, and particularly liked this kind, firm and round like a Roman's, with the hair coming to a clean-cut edge and stopping there.

"As to lovers," he went on— "I hesitate a little as to what to say about that. I'm afraid I shall shock you. Perhaps I'd better leave out that one."

"As insuperable?" she mischievously asked.

"No, as too easy," he answered.

"You'd better explain," she said.

"Well then— it's simply this: as a man— I myself admire you more because so many other men admire you. I don't sympathize with them, any!— Not for a minute. Of course, if you loved any one of them you wouldn't be my wife. But if you were my wife—"

"Well?" said she, a little breathlessly. "You're very irritating! What would you do? Kill them all? Come— If I were your wife?—"

"If you were my wife—" he turned and faced her squarely, his deep eyes blazing steadily into hers, "In the first place the more lovers you had that you didn't love the better I'd be pleased."

"And if I did?" she dared him.

"If you were my wife," he pursued with perfect quietness, "you would never love anyone else."

There was a throbbing silence.

"'Sixth— Housekeeping,'" he read.

At this she rose to her feet as if released. "Sixth and last and all-sufficient!" she burst out, giving herself a little shake as if to waken. "Final and conclusive and admitting no reply!"— I will not keep house for any man. Never! Never!! Never!!!"

"Why should you?" he said, as he had said it before; "Why not board?"

"I wouldn't board on any account!"

"But you are boarding now. Aren't you comfortable here?"

"O yes, perfectly comfortable. But this is the only boarding-house I ever saw that was comfortable."

"Why not go on as we are— if you married me?"

She laughed shrilly. "With the other boarders round them and a whole floor laid between," she parodied gaily. "No, sir! If I ever married again— and I wont— I'd want a home of my own— a whole house— and have it run as smoothly and perfectly as this does. With no more care than I have now!"

"If I could give you a whole house, like this, and run it for you as smoothly and perfectly as this one— then would you marry me?" he asked.

"O, I dare say I would," she said mockingly.

"My dear," said he, "I have kept this house— for you— for three years."

"What do you mean?" she demanded, flushingly.

"I mean that it is my business," he answered serenely. "Some men run hotels and some restaurants: I keep a number of boarding houses and make a handsome income from them. All the people are comfortable— I see to that. I planned to have you use these rooms, had the dumbwaiter run to the top so you could have meals comfortably there. You didn't much like the first housekeeper. I got one you liked better; cooks to please you, maids to please you. I have most seriously tried to make you comfortable. When you didn't like a boarder I got rid of him— or her— they are mostly all your friends now. Of course if we were married, we'd fire them all." His tone was perfectly calm and business like.

"You should keep your special apartments on top; you should also have the floor above this, a larger bedroom, drawing-room, and bath and private parlor for you;— I'd stay right here as I am now— and when you wanted me— I'd be here."

She stiffened a little at this rather tame ending. She was stirred, uneasy, dissatisfied. She felt as if something had been offered and withdrawn; something was lacking.

"It seems such a funny business— for a man," she said.

"Any funnier than Delmonico's?" he asked. "It's a business that takes some ability— witness the many failures. It is certainly useful. And it pays— amazingly."

"I thought it was real estate," she insisted.

"It is. I'm in a real estate office. I buy and sell houses— that's how I came to take this up!"

He rose up, calmly and methodically, walked over to the fire, and laid his notebook on it. "There wasn't any strength in any of those objections, my dear," said he. "Especially the first one. Previous marriage, indeed! You have never been married before. You are going to be— now."

It was some weeks after that marriage that she suddenly turned upon him— as suddenly as one can turn upon a person whose arms are about one— demanding.

"And why don't you smoke?— You never told me!"

"I shouldn't like to kiss you so well if you smoked!"— said he.

"I never had any idea," she ventured after a while, "that it could be— like this."

* * * * *

Martha's Mother

It was nine feet long. It was eight feet high. It was six feet wide. There was a closet, actually!— a closet one foot deep— that was why she took this room. There was the bed, and the trunk, and just room to open the closet door part way— that accounted for the length. There was the bed and the bureau and the chair— that accounted for the width. Between the bedside and the bureau and chair side was a strip extending the whole nine feet.

There was room to turn around by the window. There was room to turn round by the door. Martha was thin. One, two, three, four— turn. One, two, three, four— turn. She managed it nicely.

"It is a stateroom," she always said to herself. "It is a luxurious, large, well-furnished stateroom with a real window. It is not a cell."

Martha had a vigorous constructive imagination. Sometimes it was the joy of her life, her magic carpet, her Aladdin's lamp. Sometimes it frightened her— frightened her horribly, it was so strong. The cell idea had come to her one gloomy day, and she had foolishly allowed it to enter— played with it a little while. Since then she had to keep a special bar on that particular intruder, so she had arranged a stateroom "set," and forcibly kept it on hand.

Martha was a stenographer and typewriter in a real estate office. She got $12 a week, and was thankful for it. It was steady pay, and enough to live on. Seven dollars she paid for board and lodging, ninety cents for her six lunches, ten a day for carfare, including Sundays; seventy-five for laundry; one for her mother— that left one dollar and sixty-five cents for clothes, shoes, gloves, everything. She had tried cheaper board, but made up the cost in doctor's bills; and lost a good place by being ill.

"Stone walls do not a prison make, nor hall bedrooms a cage," said she determinedly. "Now then— here is another evening— what shall I do? Library? No. My eyes are tired. Besides, three times a week is enough. 'It isn't club night. Will not sit in the parlor. Too wet to walk. Can't sew, worse than reading— O good land! I'm almost ready to go with Basset!"

She shook herself and paced up and down again. Prisoners form the habit of talking to themselves— this was the suggestion that floated through her mind— that cell idea again.

"I've got to get out of this!" said Martha, stopping short. "It's enough to drive a girl crazy!" The driving process was stayed by a knock at the door. "Excuse me for coming up," said a voice. "It's Mrs. MacAvelly." Martha knew this lady well. She was a friend of Miss Podder at the Girls' Trade Union Association.

"Come in. I'm glad to see you!" she said hospitably. "Have the chair— or the bed's really more comfortable!"

"I was with Miss Podder this evening and she was anxious to know whether your union has gained any since the last meeting— I told her I'd find out— I had nothing else to do. Am I intruding?"

"Intruding!" Martha, gave a short laugh. "Why, it's a godsend, Mrs. MacAvelly! If you knew how dull the evenings are to us girls!"

"Don't you— go out much? To— to theaters— or parks?" The lady's tone was sympathetic and not inquisitive.

"Not very much," said Martha, rather sardonically. "Theaters— two girls, two dollars, and twenty cents carfare. Parks, twenty cents— walk your feet off, or sit on the benches and be stared at. Museums— not open evenings."

"But don't you have visitors— in the parlor here?"

"Did you see it?" asked Martha.

Mrs. MacAvelly had seen it. It was cold and also stuffy. It was ugly and shabby and stiff. Three tired girls sat there, two trying to read by a strangled gaslight overhead; one trying to entertain a caller in a social fiction of privacy at the other end of the room.

"Yes, we have visitors— but mostly they ask us out. And some of us don't go," said Martha darkly.

"I see, I see!" said Mrs. MacAvelly, with a pleasant smile; and Martha wondered whether she did see, or was just being civil.

"For instance, there's Mr. Basset," the girl pursued, somewhat recklessly; meaning that her visitor should understand her.

"Mr. Basset?"

"Yes, 'Pond & Basset'— one of my employers."

Mrs. MacAvelly looked pained. "Couldn't you— er— avoid it?" she suggested.

"You mean shake him?" asked Martha. "Why, yes— I could. Might lose my job. Get another place— another Basset, probably."

"I see!" said Mrs. MacAvelly again. "Like the Fox and the Swarm of Flies! There ought to be a more comfortable way of living for all you girls! And how about the union— I have to be going back to Miss Podder."

Martha gave her the information she wanted, and started to accompany her downstairs. They heard the thin jangle of the door-bell, down through the echoing halls, and the dragging feet of the servant coming up. A kinky black head was thrust in at the door.

"Mr. Basset, calling on Miss Joyce," was announced formally. Martha stiffened. "Please tell Mr. Basset I am not feeling well tonight— and beg to be excused.”

She looked rather defiantly at her guest, as Lucy clattered down the long stairs; then stole to the railing and peered down the narrow well. She heard the message given with pompous accuracy, and then heard the clear, firm tones of Mr. Basset: "Tell Miss Joyce that I will wait."

Martha returned to her room in three long steps, slipped off her shoes and calmly got into bed. "Good-night, Mrs. MacAvelly," she said. "I'm so sorry, but my head aches and I've gone to bed! Would you be so very good as to tell Lucy so as you're going down." Mrs. MacAvelly said she would, and departed, and Martha lay conscientiously quiet till she heard the door shut far below. She was quiet, but she was not contented.

Yet the discontent of Martha was as nothing to the discontent of Mrs. Joyce, her mother, in her rural home. Here was a woman of fifty-three, alert, vigorous, nervously active; but an agitated horse had danced upon her, and her usefulness, as she understood it, was over.

She could not get about without crutches, nor use her hands for needlework, though still able to write after a fashion. Writing was not her forte, however, at the best of times. She lived with a widowed sister in a little, lean dusty farmhouse by the side of the road; a hill road that went nowhere in particular, and was too steep for those who were going there. Brisk on her crutches, Mrs. Joyce hopped about the little house, there was nowhere else to hop to. She had talked her sister out long since— Mary never had much to say. Occasionally they quarreled and then Mrs. Joyce hopped only in her room, a limited process.

She sat at the window one day, staring greedily out at the lumpy rock-ribbed road; silent, perforce, and tapping the arms of her chair with nervous intensity. Suddenly she called out, "Mary! Mary Ames! Come here quick! There's somebody coming up the road!"

Mary came in, as fast as she could with eggs in her apron. "It's Mrs. Holmes!" she said. "And a boarder, I guess."

"No, it ain't," said Mrs. Joyce, eagerly. "It's that woman that's visiting the Holmes— she was in church last week, Myra Slater told me about her. Her name's MacDowell, or something."

"It ain't MacDowell," said her sister. "I remember; it's MacAvelly." This theory was borne out by Mrs. Holmes' entrance and introduction of her friend.

"Have you any eggs for us, Mrs. Ames?" she said.

"Set down— set down," said Mrs. Ames cordially. "I was just getting in my eggs— but here's only about eight yet. How many do you want?"

"I want all you can find," said Mrs. Holmes. "Two dozen, three dozen— all I can carry."

"There's two hens laying out— I'll go and look them up. And I ain't been in the woodshed chamber yet. I'll go and hunt. You set right here with my sister." And Mrs. Ames bustled off.

"Pleasant view you have here," said Mrs. MacAvelly politely, while Mrs. Holmes rocked and fanned herself.

"Pleasant! Glad you think so, ma'am. Maybe you city folks wouldn't think so much of views if you had nothing else to look at!"

"What would you like to look at?"

"Folks!" said Mrs. Joyce briefly. "Lots of folks! Something doing."

"You'd like to live in the city?"

"Yes, ma'am— I would so! I worked in the city once when I was a girl. Waitress. In a big restaurant. I got to be cashier— in two years! I like the business!"

"And then you married a farmer?" suggested Mrs. Holmes.

"Yes, I did. And I never was sorry, Mrs. Holmes. David Joyce was a mighty good man. We were engaged before I left home— I was working to help earn, so that we could marry."

"There's plenty of work on a farm, isn't there?" Mrs. MacAvelly inquired.

Mrs. Joyce's eager eyes kindled. "There is so!" she agreed. "Lots to do. And lots to manage! We kept help then, and the farm hands, and the children growing up. And some seasons we took boarders."

"Did you like that?"

"I did. I liked it first rate. I like lots of people, and to do for them. The best time I ever had was one summer I ran a hotel."

"Ran a hotel! How interesting!"

"Yes— it was interesting! I had a cousin who kept a summer hotel up here in the mountains and he was short handed that summer and got me to go up and help him out. Then he was taken sick, and I had the whole thing on my shoulders! I just enjoyed it! And the place cleared more that summer than it ever did! He said it was owing to his advantageous buying. Maybe it was! But I could have bought more advantageous than he did— I could have told him that. Point of fact, I did tell him that— and he wouldn't have me again."

"That was a pity!" said Mrs. Holmes. "And I suppose if it wasn't for your foot you would do that now— and enjoy it!"

"Of course I could!" protested Mrs. Joyce. "Do it better than ever, city or country! But here I am, tied by the leg! And dependent on my sister and children! It galls me terribly!"

Mrs. Holmes nodded sympathetically. "You are very brave, Mrs. Joyce," she said. "I admire your courage, and—" she couldn't say patience, so she said, "cheerfulness."

Mrs. Ames came in with more eggs. "Not enough, but some," she said, and the visitors departed therewith.

Toward the end of the summer, Miss Podder at the Girls' Trade Union Association, sweltering in the little office, was pleased to receive a call from her friend, Mrs. MacAvelly.

"I'd no idea you were in town," she said.

"I'm not, officially," answered her visitor, "just stopping over between visits. It's hotter than I thought it would be, even on the upper west side."

"Think what it is on the lower east side!" answered Miss Podder, eagerly. "Hot all day— and hot at night! My girls do suffer so! They are so crowded!"

"How do the clubs get on?" asked Mrs. MacAvelly. "Have your girls any residence clubs yet?"

"No— nothing worth while. It takes somebody to run it right, you know. The girls can't; the people who work for money can't meet our wants— and the people who work for love, don't work well as a rule."

Mrs. McAvelly smiled sympathetically. "You're quite right about that," she said. "But really— some of those 'Homes' are better than others, aren't they?"

"The girls hate them," answered Miss Podder. "They'd rather board— even two or three in a room. They like their

65

independence. You remember Martha Joyce?"

Mrs. MacAvelly remembered. "Yes," she said, "I do— I met her mother this summer."

"She's a cripple, isn't she?" asked Miss Podder. "Martha's told me about her."

"Why, not exactly. She's what a Westerner might call 'crippled up some,' but she's livelier than most well persons." And she amused her friend with a vivid rehearsal of Mrs. Joyce's love of the city and her former triumphs in restaurant and hotel.

"She'd be a fine one to run such a house for the girls, wouldn't she?" suddenly cried Miss Podder.

"Why— if she could," Mrs. MacAvelly admitted slowly.

"Could! Why not? You say she gets about easily enough. All she's have to do is manage, you see. She could order by phone and keep the servants running!"

"I'm sure she'd like it," said Mrs. MacAvelly. "But don't such things require capital?"

Miss Podder was somewhat daunted. "Yes— some; but I guess we could raise it. If we could find the right house!"

"Let's look in the paper," suggested her visitor. "I've got a Herald."

"There's one that reads all right," Miss Podder proclaimed. "The location's good, and it's got a lot of rooms— furnished. I suppose it would cost too much."

Mrs. MacAvelly agreed, rather ruefully. "Come," she said, "it's time to close here, surely. Let's go and look at that house, anyway. It's not far."

They got their permit and were in the house very shortly. "I remember this place," said Miss Podder. "It was for sale earlier in the summer."

It was one of those once spacious houses, not of "old," but at least of "middle-aged" New York; with large rooms arbitrarily divided into smaller ones.

"It's been a boarding-house, that's clear," said Mrs. MacAvelly.

"Why, of course," Miss Podder answered, eagerly plunging about and examining everything. "Anybody could see that! But it's been done over— most thoroughly. The cellar's all whitewashed, and there's a new furnace, and new range, and look at this icebox!" It was an ice-closet, as a matter of fact, of large capacity, and a most sanitary aspect.

"Isn't it too big?" Mrs. MacAvelly inquired.

"Not for a boarding-house, my dear," Miss Podder enthusiastically replied. "Why, they could buy a side of beef with that ice-box! And look at the extra ovens! Did you ever see a place better furnished— for what we want? It looks as if it had been done on purpose!"

"It does, doesn't it?" said Mrs. MacAvelley.

Miss Podder, eager and determined, let no grass grow under her feet. The rent of the place was within reason. "If they had twenty boarders— and some "mealers," I believe it could be done! she said. "It's a miracle— this house. Seems as if somebody had done it just for us!"

Armed with a list of girls who would agree to come, for six and seven dollars a week, Miss Podder made a trip to Willettville and laid the matter before Martha's mother.

"What an outrageous rent!" said that lady.

"Yes— New York rents are rather inconsiderate," Miss Podder admitted. "But see, here's a guaranteed income if the girls stay— and I'm sure they will; and if the cooking's good you could easily get table boarders besides."

Mrs. Joyce hopped to the bureau and brought out a hard, sharp-pointed pencil, and a lined writing tablet. "Let's figure it out," said she. "You say that house rents furnished at $3,200. It would take a cook and a chambermaid!"

"And a furnace man," said Miss Podder. "They come to about fifty a year. The cook would be thirty a month, the maid twenty-five, if you got first-class help, and you'd need it."

"That amounts to $710 altogether," stated Mrs. Joyce.

"Fuel and light and such things would be $200," Miss Podder estimated, "and I think you ought to allow $200 more for breakage and extras generally."

"That's $4,310 already," said Mrs. Joyce.

Then there's the food," Miss Podder went on. "How much do you think it would cost to feed twenty girls, two meals a day, and three Sundays?"

"And three more," Mrs. Joyce added, "with me, and the help, twenty-three. I could do it for $2.00 a week apiece."

"Oh!" said Miss Podder. "Could you? At New York prices?"

"See me do it!" said Mrs. Joyce.

"That makes a total expense of $6,710 a year. Now, what's the income, ma'am?"

The income was clear— if they could get it. Ten girls at $6.00

and ten at $7.00 made $130.00 a week— $6,700.00 a year.

"There you are!" said Mrs. Joyce triumphantly. "And the 'mealers'— if my griddle-cakes don't fetch them I'm mistaken! If I have ten— at $5.00 a week and clear $3.00 off them— that'll be another bit— $1,560 more. Total income $8,320. More than one thousand clear! Maybe I can feed them a little higher— or charge less!"

The two women worked together for an hour or so; Mrs. Ames drawn in later with demands as to butter, eggs, and "eating chickens."

"There's an ice-box as big as a closet," said Miss Podder.

Mrs. Joyce smiled triumphantly. "Good!" she said. "I can buy my critters of Judson here and have him freight them down. I can get apples here and potatoes, and lots of stuff."

"You'll probably need a little capital to start with," suggested Miss Podder. "I think the Association could—"

"It don't have to, thank you just the same," said Mrs. Joyce. "I've got enough in my stocking to take me to New York and get some fuel. Besides, all my boarders are going to pay in advance— that's the one sure way. The mealers can buy tickets!" Her eyes danced. She fairly coursed about the room on her nimble crutches. "My!" she said, "it will seem good to have my girl to feed again."

The house opened in September, full of eager girls with large appetites long unsatisfied. The place was new-smelling, fresh-painted, beautifully clean. The furnishing was cheap, but fresh, tasteful, with minor conveniences dear to the hearts of women. The smallest rooms were larger than hall bedrooms, the big ones were shared by friends. Martha and her mother had a chamber with two beds and space to spare!

The dining-room was very large, and at night the tables were turned into "settles" by the wall and the girls could dance to the sound of a hired pianola. So could the "mealers," when invited; and there was soon a waiting list of both sexes.

"I guess I can make a living," said Mrs. Joyce, "allowing for bad years."

"I don't understand how you feed us so well— for so little," said Miss Podder, who was one of the boarders.

"'Sh!" said Mrs. Joyce, privately. "Your breakfast don't really cost more than ten cents— nor your dinner fifteen— not the way I order! Things taste good because they're cooked good— that's all!"

"And you have no troubles with your help?"

"'Sh!" said Mrs. Joyce again, more privately. "I work them hard — and pay them a bonus— a dollar a week extra, as long as they give satisfaction. It reduces my profits some— but it's worth it!"

"It's worth it to us, I'm sure!" said Miss Podder.

Mrs. MacAvelly called one evening in the first week, with warm interest and approval. The tired girls were sitting about in comfortable rockers and lounges, under comfortable lights, reading and sewing. The untired ones were dancing in the dining-room, to the industrious pianola, or having games of cards in the parlor.

"Do you think it'll be a success?" she asked her friend.

"It is a success!" Miss Podder triumphantly replied. "I'm immensely proud of it!"

"I should think you would be," said Mrs. MacAvelly.

The doorbell rang sharply. Mrs. Joyce was hopping through the hall at the moment, and promptly opened it.

"Does Miss Martha Joyce board here?" inquired a gentleman.

"She does."

"I should like to see her," said he, handing in his card.

Mrs. Joyce read the card and looked at the man, her face setting in hard lines. She had heard that name before.

"Miss Joyce is engaged," she replied curtly, still holding the door. He could see past her into the bright, pleasant rooms. He heard the music below, the swing of dancing feet, Martha's cheerful laugh from the parlor. The little lady on crutches blocked his path.

"Are you the housekeeper of this place?" he asked sharply.

"I'm more than that!" she answered. "I'm Martha's mother."

Mr. Basset concluded he would not wait.

* * * * *

Charlotte Gilman

Three Thanksgivings

Andrew's letter and Jean's letter were in Mrs. Morrison's lap. She had read them both, and sat looking at them with a varying sort of smile, now motherly and now unmotherly.

"You belong with me," Andrew wrote. "It is not right that Jean's husband should support my mother. I can do it easily now. You shall have a good room and every comfort. The old house will let for enough to give you quite a little income of your own, or it can be sold and I will invest the money where you'll get a deal more out of it. It is not right that you should live alone there. Sally is old and liable to accident. I am anxious about you. Come on for Thanksgiving— and come to stay. Here is the money to come with. You know I want you. Annie joins me in sending love. *Andrew*."

Mrs. Morrison read it all through again, and laid it down with her quiet, twinkling smile. Then she read Jean's.

"Now, mother, you've got to come to us for Thanksgiving this year. Just think! You haven't seen baby since he was three months old! And have never seen the twins. You won't know him — he's such a splendid big boy now.

Joe says for you to come, of course. And, mother, why won't you come and live with us? Joe wants you, too. There's the little room upstairs; it's not very big, but we can put in a Franklin stove for you and make you pretty comfortable. Joe says he should think you ought to sell that white elephant of a place. He says he could put the money into his store and pay you good interest. I wish you would, mother. We'd just love to have you here. You'd be such a comfort to me, and such a help with the babies. And Joe just loves you. Do come now, and stay with us. Here is the money for the trip. —Your affectionate daughter, *Jeannie*."

Mrs. Morrison laid this beside the other, folded both, and placed them in their respective envelopes, then in their several well-filled pigeon-holes in her big, old-fashioned desk. She turned and paced slowly up and down the long parlor, a tall woman, commanding of respect, yet of a winningly attractive manner, erect and light-footed, still imposingly handsome.

It was now November, the last lingering boarder was long since gone, and a quiet winter lay before her. She was alone, but for Sally; and she smiled at Andrew's cautious expression, "liable to accident." He could not say "feeble" or "ailing," Sally being a colored lady of changeless aspect and incessant activity.

Mrs. Morrison was alone, and while living in the Welcome House she was never unhappy. Her father had built it, she was born there, she grew up playing on the broad green lawns in front, and in the acre of garden behind. It was the finest house in the village, and she then thought it the finest in the world. Even after living with her father at Washington and abroad, after visiting hall, castle and palace, she still found the Welcome House beautiful and impressive.

If she kept on taking boarders she could live the year through, and pay interest, but not principal, on her little mortgage. This had been the one possible and necessary thing while the children were there, though it was a business she hated. But her youthful experience in diplomatic circles, and the years of practical management in church affairs, enabled her to bear it with patience and success. The boarders often confided to one another, as they chatted and tatted on the long piazza, that Mrs. Morrison was "certainly very refined."

Now Sally whisked in cheerfully, announcing supper, and Mrs. Morrison went out to her great silver tea-tray at the lit end of the long, dark mahogany table, with as much dignity as if twenty titled guests were before her. Afterward Mr. Butts called. He came early in the evening, with his usual air of determination and a somewhat unusual spruceness. Mr. Peter Butts was a florid, blonde person, a little stout, a little pompous, sturdy and immovable in the attitude of a self-made man. He had been a poor boy when she was a rich girl; and it gratified him much to realize— and to call upon her to realize— that their positions had changed. He meant no unkindness, his pride was honest and unveiled. Tact he had none.

She had refused Mr. Butts, almost with laughter, when he proposed to her in her gay girlhood. She had refused him, more gently, when he proposed to her in her early widowhood. He had always been her friend, and her husband's friend, a solid member of the church, and had taken the small mortgage of the house. She refused to allow him at first, but he was convincingly frank about it.

"This has nothing to do with my wanting you, Delia Morrison," he said. "I've always wanted you— and I've always wanted this house, too. You won't sell, but you've got to mortgage. By and by you can't pay up, and I'll get it— see? Then maybe you'll take me — to keep the house. Don't be a fool, Delia. It's a perfectly good investment."

She had taken the loan. She had paid the interest. She would pay the interest if she had to take boarders all her life. And she would not, at any price, marry Peter Butts.

He broached the subject again that evening, cheerful and undismayed. "You might as well come to it, Delia," he said. "Then we could live right here just the same. You aren't so young as you were, to be sure; I'm not, either. But you are as good a housekeeper as ever— better— you've had more experience."

"You are extremely kind, Mr. Butts," said the lady, "but I do not wish to marry you."

"I know you don't," he said. "You've made that clear. You don't, but I do. You've had your way and married the minister. He was a good man, but he's dead. Now you might as well marry me."

"I do not wish to marry again, Mr. Butts; neither you nor anyone."

"Very proper, very proper, Delia," he replied. "It wouldn't look well if you did— at any rate, if you showed it. But why shouldn't you? The children are gone now— you can't hold them up against me any more."

"Yes, the children are both settled now, and doing nicely," she admitted.

"You don't want to go and live with them— either one of them — do you?" he asked.

"I should prefer to stay here," she answered.

"Exactly! And you can't! You'd rather live here and be a grandee— but you can't do it. Keeping house for boarders isn't any better than keeping house for me, as I see. You'd much better marry me."

"I should prefer to keep the house without you, Mr. Butts."

"I know you would. But you can't, I tell you. I'd like to know what a woman of your age can do with a house like this— and no money? You can't live eternally on hens' eggs and garden truck. That won't pay the mortgage."

Mrs. Morrison looked at him with her cordial smile, calm and non-committal. "Perhaps I can manage it," she said.

"That mortgage falls due two years from Thanksgiving, you know."

"Yes— I have not forgotten."

"Well, then, you might just as well marry me now, and save two years of interest. It'll be my house, either way— but you'll be keeping it just the same."

"It is very kind of you, Mr. Butts. I must decline the offer none the less. I can pay the interest, I am sure. And perhaps— in two years' time— I can pay the principal. It's not a large sum."

"That depends on how you look at it," said he. "Two thousand dollars is considerable money for a single woman to raise in two years— and interest."

He went away, as cheerful and determined as ever; and Mrs. Morrison saw him go with a keen, light in her fine eyes, a more definite line to that steady, pleasant smile. Then she went to spend Thanksgiving with Andrew. He was glad to see her. Annie was glad to see her. They proudly installed her in "her room," and said she must call it "home" now.

This affectionately offered home was twelve by fifteen, and eight feet high. It had two windows, one looking at some pale gray clapboards within reach of a broom, the other giving a view of several small fenced yards occupied by cats, clothes and children. There was an ailanthus tree under the window, a lady ailanthus tree. Annie told her how profusely it bloomed.

Mrs. Morrison particularly disliked the smell of ailanthus flowers. "It doesn't bloom in November," said she to herself. "I can be thankful for that!"

Andrew's church was very like the church of his father, and Mrs. Andrew was doing her best to fill the position of minister's wife— doing it well, too— there was no vacancy for a minister's mother. Besides, the work she had done so cheerfully to help her husband was not what she most cared for, after all. She liked the people, she liked to manage, but she was not strong on doctrine. Even her husband had never known how far her views differed from his. Mrs. Morrison had never mentioned what they were.

Andrew's people were very polite to her. She was invited out with them, waited upon and watched over and set down among the old ladies and gentlemen— she had never realized so keenly that she was no longer young. Here nothing recalled her youth, every careful provision anticipated age. Annie brought her a hot-water bag at night, tucking it in at the foot of the bed with affectionate care. Mrs. Morrison thanked her, and subsequently took it out— airing the bed a little before she got into it. The house seemed very hot to her, after the big, windy halls at home.

The little dining-room, the little round table with the little round fern-dish in the middle, the little turkey and the little carving-set— game-set she would have called it— all made her feel as if she was looking through the wrong end of an opera-glass.

In Annie's precise efficiency she saw no room for her assistance; no room in the church, no room in the small, busy town, prosperous and progressive, and no room in the house.

"Not enough to turn round in!" she said to herself. Annie, who had grown up in a city flat, thought their little parsonage palatial. Mrs. Morrison grew up in the Welcome House. She stayed a week, pleasant and polite, conversational, interested in all that went on.

"I think your mother is just lovely," said Annie to Andrew.

"Charming woman, your mother," said the leading church member.

"What a delightful old lady your mother is!" said the pretty soprano.

Andrew was deeply hurt and disappointed when she announced her determination to stay on for the present in her old home. "Dear boy," she said, "you mustn't take it to heart. I love to be with you, of course, but I love my home, and want to keep it as long as I can. It is a great pleasure to see you and Annie so well settled, and so happy together. I am most truly thankful for you."

"My home is open to you whenever you wish to come, mother," said Andrew. But he was a little angry.

Mrs. Morrison came home as eager as a girl, and opened her own door with her own key, in spite of Sally's haste. Two years were before her in which she must find some way to keep herself and Sally, and to pay two thousand dollars and the interest to Peter Butts.

She considered her assets. There was the house— the white elephant. It was big— very big. It was profusely furnished. Her father had entertained lavishly like the Southern-born, hospitable gentleman he was; and the bedrooms ran in suites— somewhat deteriorated by the use of boarders, but still numerous and habitable. Boarders— she abhorred them. They were people from afar, strangers and interlopers. She went over the place from garret to cellar, from front gate to backyard fence. The garden had great possibilities. She was fond of gardening and understood it well. She measured and estimated.

"This garden," she finally decided, "with the hens, will feed us two women and sell enough to pay Sally. If we make plenty of jelly, it may cover the coal bill, too. As to clothes— I don't need any. They last admirably. I can manage. I can live— but two thousand dollars— and interest!"

In the great attic was more furniture, discarded sets put there when her extravagant young mother had ordered new ones. And chairs— uncounted chairs. Senator Welcome used to invite numbers to meet his political friends— and they had delivered glowing orations in the wide, double parlors, the impassioned speakers standing on a temporary dais, now in the cellar; and the enthusiastic listeners disposed more or less comfortably on these serried rows of "folding chairs," which folded sometimes, and let down the visitor in scarlet confusion to the floor. She sighed as she remembered those vivid days and glittering nights. She used to steal downstairs in her little pink wrapper and listen to the eloquence. It delighted her young soul to see her father rising on his toes, coming down sharply on his heels, hammering one hand upon the other; and then to hear the fusilade of applause.

Here were the chairs, often borrowed for weddings, funerals, and church affairs, somewhat worn and depleted, but still numerous. She mused upon them. Chairs— hundreds of chairs. They would sell for very little. She went through her linen room. A splendid stock in the old days; always carefully washed by Sally; surviving even the boarders. Plenty of bedding, plenty of towels, plenty of napkins and tablecloths. "It would make a good hotel— but I can't have it so— I can't! Besides, there's no need of another hotel here. The poor little Haskins House is never full."

The stock in the china closet was more damaged than some other things, naturally; but she inventoried it with care. The countless cups of crowded church receptions were especially prominent. Later additions these, not very costly cups, but numerous, appallingly.

When she had her long list of assets all in order, she sat and studied it with a clear and daring mind. Hotel— boarding-house— she could think of nothing else. School! A girls' school! A boarding school! There was money to be made at that, and fine work done. It was a brilliant thought at first, and she gave several hours, and much paper and ink, to its full consideration. But she would need some capital for advertising; she must engage teachers— adding to her definite obligation; and to establish it, well, it would require time. Mr. Butts, obstinate, pertinacious, oppressively affectionate, would give her no time. He meant to force her to marry him for her own good— and his.

She shrugged her fine shoulders with a little shiver. Marry Peter Butts! Never! Mrs. Morrison still loved her husband. Some day she meant to see him again— God willing— and she did not wish to have to tell him that at fifty she had been driven into marrying Peter Butts.

Better live with Andrew. Yet when she thought of living with Andrew, she shivered again. Pushing back her sheets of figures and lists of personal property, she rose to her full graceful height and began to walk the floor. There was plenty of floor to walk. She considered, with a set deep thoughtfulness, the town and the townspeople, the surrounding country, the hundreds upon hundreds of women whom she knew— and liked, and who liked her. It used to be said of Senator Welcome that he had no enemies; and some people, strangers, maliciously disposed, thought it no credit to his character. His daughter had no enemies, but no one had ever blamed her for her unlimited friendliness. In her father's wholesale entertainments the whole town knew and admired his daughter; in her husband's popular church she had come to know the women of the countryside.

Her mind strayed off to these women, farmers' wives, comfortably off in a plain way, but starving for companionship, for occasional stimulus and pleasure. It was one of her joys in her husband's time to bring together these women— to teach and entertain them. Suddenly she stopped short in the middle of the great high-ceiled room, and drew her head up proudly like a victorious queen. One wide, triumphant, sweeping glance she cast at the well-loved walls— and went back to her desk, working swiftly, excitedly, well into the hours of the night.

Soon the little town began to buzz, and the murmur ran far out into the surrounding country. Sunbonnets wagged over fences; butcher carts and pedlar's wagon carried the news farther; and ladies visiting found one topic in a thousand houses. Mrs. Morrison was going to entertain. Mrs. Morrison had invited the whole feminine population, it would appear, to meet Mrs. Isabelle Carter Blake, of Chicago. Even Haddleton had heard of Mrs. Isabelle Carter Blake. And even Haddleton had nothing but admiration for her. She was known the world over for her splendid work for children— for the school children and the working children of the country. Yet she was known also to have lovingly and wisely reared six children of her own— and made her husband happy in his home. On top of that she had lately written a novel, a popular novel, of which everyone was talking; and on top of that she was an intimate friend of a certain conspicuous Countess— an Italian. It was even rumored, by some who knew Mrs. Morrison better than others— or thought they did— that the Countess was coming, too!

No one had known before that Delia Welcome was a school-mate of Isabel Carter, and a lifelong friend; and that was ground for talk in itself.

The day arrived, and the guests arrived. They came in hundreds upon hundreds, and found ample room in the great white house. The highest dream of the guests was realized— the Countess had come, too. With excited joy they met her, receiving impressions that would last them for all their lives, for those large widening waves of reminiscence which delight us the more as years pass. It was an incredible glory— Mrs. Isabelle Carter Blake, and a Countess!

Some were moved to note that Mrs. Morrison looked the easy peer of these eminent ladies, and treated the foreign nobility precisely as she did her other friends. She spoke, her clear quiet voice reaching across the murmuring din, and silencing it.

"Shall we go into the east room? If you will all take chairs in the east room, Mrs. Blake is going to be so kind as to address us. Also perhaps her friend—"

They crowded in, sitting somewhat timorously on the unfolded chairs. Then the great Mrs. Blake made them an address of memorable power and beauty, which received vivid sanction from that imposing presence in Parisian garments on the platform by her side.

Mrs. Blake spoke to them of the work she was interested in, and how it was aided everywhere by the women's clubs. She gave them the number of these clubs, and described with contagious enthusiasm the inspiration of their great meetings. She spoke of the women's club houses, going up in city after city, where many associations meet and help one another. She was winning and convincing and most entertaining— an extremely attractive speaker.

Had they a women's club there? They had not. Not yet, she suggested, adding that it took no time at all to make one. They were delighted and impressed with Mrs. Blake's speech, but its effect was greatly intensified by the address of the Countess.

"I, too, am American," she told them; "born here, reared in England, married in Italy." And she stirred their hearts with a vivid account of the women's clubs and associations all over Europe, and what they were accomplishing.

She was going back soon, she said, the wiser and happier for this visit to her native land, and she should remember particularly this beautiful, quiet town, trusting that if she came to it again it would have joined the great sisterhood of women, "whose hands were touching around the world for the common good."

It was a great occasion. The Countess left next day, but Mrs. Blake remained, and spoke in some of the church meetings, to an ever widening circle of admirers. Her suggestions were practical.

"What you need here is a 'Rest and Improvement Club,'" she said. "Here are all you women coming in from the country to do your shopping— and no place to go to. No place to lie down if you're tired, to meet a friend, to eat your lunch in peace, to do your hair. All you have to do is organize, pay some small regular due, and provide yourselves with what you want."

There was a volume of questions and suggestions, a little opposition, much random activity. Who was to do it? Where was there a suitable place? They would have to hire someone to take charge of it. It would only be used once a week. It would cost too much.

Mrs. Blake, still practical, made another suggestion. Why not combine business with pleasure, and make use of the best place in town, if you can get it? I think Mrs. Morrison could be persuaded to let you use part of her house; it's quite too big for one woman."

Then Mrs. Morrison, simple and cordial as ever, greeted with warm enthusiasm by her wide circle of friends.

"I have been thinking this over," she said. "Mrs. Blake has been discussing it with me. My house is certainly big enough for all of you, and there am I, with nothing to do but entertain you. Suppose you formed such a club as you speak of— for Rest and Improvement. My parlors are big enough for all manner of meetings; there are bedrooms in plenty for resting. If you form such a club I shall be glad to help with my great, cumbersome house, shall be delighted to see so many friends there so often; and I think I could furnish accommodations more cheaply than you could manage in any other way."

Then Mrs. Blake gave them facts and figures, showing how much clubhouses cost— and how little this arrangement would cost.

"Most women have very little money, I know," she said, "and they hate to spend it on themselves when they have; but even a little money from each goes a long way when it is put together. I fancy there are none of us so poor we could not squeeze out, say ten cents a week. For a hundred women that would be ten dollars. Could you feed a hundred tired women for ten dollars, Mrs. Morrison?"

Mrs. Morrison smiled cordially. "Not on chicken pie," she said, "But I could give them tea and coffee, crackers and cheese for that, I think. And a quiet place to rest, and a reading room, and a place to hold meetings."

Then Mrs. Blake quite swept them off their feet by her wit and eloquence. She gave them to understand that if a share in the palatial accommodation of the Welcome House, and as good tea and coffee as old Sally made, with a place to meet, a place to rest, a place to talk, a place to lie down, could be had for ten cents a week each, she advised them to clinch the arrangement at once before Mrs. Morrison's natural good sense had overcome her enthusiasm.

Before Mrs. Isabelle Carter Blake had left, Haddleton had a large and eager women's club, whose entire expenses, outside of stationary and postage, consisted of ten cents a week per capita, paid to Mrs. Morrison. Everybody belonged. It was open at once for charter members, and all pressed forward to claim that privileged place. They joined by hundreds, and from each member came this tiny sum to Mrs. Morrison each week. It was very little money, taken separately. But it added up with silent speed.

Tea and coffee, purchased in bulk, crackers by the barrel, and whole cheeses— these are not expensive luxuries. The town was full of Mrs. Morrison's ex-Sunday-school boys, who furnished her with the best they had— at cost.

There was a good deal of work, a good deal of care, and room for the whole supply of Mrs. Morrison's diplomatic talent and experience. Saturdays found the Welcome House as full as it could hold, and Sundays found Mrs. Morrison in bed. But she liked it.

A busy, hopeful year flew by, and then she went to Jean's for Thanksgiving. The room Jean gave her was about the same size as her haven in Andrew's home, but one flight higher up, and with a sloping ceiling. Mrs. Morrison whitened her dark hair upon it, and rubbed her head confusedly. Then she shook it with renewed determination.

The house was full of babies. There was little Joe, able to get about, and into everything. There were the twins, and there was the new baby. There was one servant, over-worked and cross. There was a small, cheap, totally inadequate nursemaid. There was Jean, happy but tired, full of joy, anxiety and affection, proud of her children, proud of her husband, and delighted to unfold her heart to her mother.

By the hour she babbled of their cares and hopes, while Mrs. Morrison, tall and elegant in her well-kept old black silk, sat holding the baby or trying to hold the twins. The old silk was pretty well finished by the week's end.

Joseph talked to her also, telling her how well he was getting on, and how much he needed capital, urging her to come and stay with them; it was such a help to Jeannie; asking questions about the house.

There was no going visiting here. Jeannie could not leave the babies. And few visitors; all the little suburb being full of similarly overburdened mothers. Such as called found Mrs. Morrison charming. What she found them, she did not say. She bade her daughter an affectionate goodbye when the week was up, smiling at their mutual contentment.

"Goodbye, my dear children," she said. "I am so glad for all your happiness. I am thankful for both of you." But she was more thankful to get home.

Mr. Butts did not have to call for his interest this time, but he called none the less. "How on earth did you get it, Delia?" he demanded. "Screwed it out of these club women?"

"Your interest is so moderate, Mr. Butts, that it is easier to meet than you imagine," was her answer. "Do you know the average interest they charge in Colorado? The women vote there, you know."

He went away with no more personal information than that; and no nearer approach to the twin goals of his desire than the passing of the year.

"One more year, Delia," he said; "then you'll have to give in."

"One more year!" she said to herself, and took up her chosen task with renewed energy. The financial basis of the undertaking was very simple, but it would never have worked so well under less skillful management. Five dollars a year these country women could not have faced, but ten cents a week was possible to the poorest. There was no difficulty in collecting, for they brought it themselves; no unpleasantness in receiving, for old Sally stood at the receipt of custom and presented the covered cash box when they came for their tea. On the crowded Saturdays the great urns were set going, the mighty array of cups arranged in easy reach, the ladies filed by, each taking her refection and leaving her dime.

Where the effort came was in enlarging the membership and keeping up the attendance, and this effort was precisely in the line of Mrs. Morrison's splendid talents. Serene, cheerful, inconspicuously active, planning like the born statesman she was, executing like a practical politician, Mrs. Morrison gave her mind to the work, and thrived upon it. Circle within circle, and group within group, she set small classes and departments at work, having a boys' club by and by in the big room over the woodshed, girls' clubs, reading clubs, study clubs, little meetings of every sort that were not held in churches, and some that were — previously. For each and all there was, if wanted, tea and coffee, crackers and cheese; simple fare, of unvarying excellence, and from each and all, into the little cash box, ten cents for these refreshments. From the club members this came weekly; and the club members, kept up by a constant variety of interests, came every week. As to numbers, before the first six months was over The Haddleton Rest and Improvement Club numbered five hundred women.

Now, five hundred times ten cents a week is twenty-six hundred dollars a year. Twenty-six hundred dollars a year would not be very much to build or rent a large house, to furnish five hundred people with chairs, lounges, books, and magazines, dishes and service; and with food and drink even of the simplest. But if you are miraculously supplied with a club-house, furnished, with a manager and servant on the spot, then that amount of money goes a long way.

On Saturdays Mrs. Morrison hired two helpers for half a day, for half a dollar each. She stocked the library with many magazines for fifty dollars a year. She covered fuel, light, and small miscellanies with another hundred. And she fed her multitude with the plain viands agreed upon, at about four cents apiece.

For her collateral entertainments, her many visits, the various new expenses entailed, she paid as well; and yet at the end of the first year she had not only her interest, but a solid thousand dollars of clear profit. With a calm smile she surveyed it, heaped in neat stacks of bills in the small safe in the wall behind her bed. Even Sally did not know it was there.

The second season was better than the first. There were difficulties, excitements, even some opposition, but she rounded out the year triumphantly. "After that," she said to herself, "they may have the deluge if they like."

She made all expenses, made her interest, made a little extra cash, clearly her own, all over and above the second thousand dollars. Then she wrote to son and daughter, inviting them and their families to come home to Thanksgiving, and closing each letter with joyous pride: "Here is the money to come with."

They all came, with all the children and two nurses. There was plenty of room in the Welcome House, and plenty of food on the long mahogany table. Sally was as brisk as a bee, brilliant in scarlet and purple; Mrs. Morrison carved her big turkey with queenly grace.

"I don't see that you're over-run with club women, mother," said Jeannie.

"It's Thanksgiving, you know; they're all at home. I hope they are all as happy, as thankful for their homes as I am for mine," said Mrs. Morrison.

Afterward Mr. Butts called. With dignity and calm unruffled, Mrs. Morrison handed him his interest— and principal. Mr. Butts was almost loath to receive it, though his hand automatically grasped the crisp blue check.

"I didn't know you had a bank account," he protested, somewhat dubiously.

"Oh, yes; you'll find the check will be honored, Mr. Butts."

"I'd like to know how you got this money. You can't have skinned it out of that club of yours."

"I appreciate your friendly interest, Mr. Butts; you have been most kind."

"I believe some of these great friends of yours have lent it to you. You won't be any better off, I can tell you."

"Come, come, Mr. Butts! Don't quarrel with good money. Let us part friends."

And they parted.

* * * * *

Charlotte Gilman

The Barrel

I was walking, peacefully enough, along a plain ordinary road, when I lifted my head and observed an impressive gateway. The pillars were of stone, high, carven, massive; mighty gates of wrought iron hung between them, the gray wall stretched away on either side.

As the gates were open and there was no prohibitory sign, I entered, and for easy miles walked on; under the springing arches of tall elms, flat roofs of beech, and level fans of fir and pine; through woodland, park and meadow, with glimpses of starred lily-ponds, blue lakelets, and bright brooks; seeing the dappled deer, the swans and pheasants— a glorious place indeed.

Then a smooth turn, and across velvet lawns and statued gardens I saw a towering palace, so nobly beautiful, so majestic, I took off my hat involuntarily. Approaching it, I was met by courteous servingmen; told that it was open to visitors; and shown from hall to hall, from floor to floor; where every object was a work of art; where line, color and proportion, perfect architecture and fitting decoration made an overwhelming beauty.

"Whose it is?" I inquired. "Some Duke?— King?— Emperor? Who owns this palace?— this glorious estate?" They bowed and offered to lead me to him.

Downward and toward the back; through servants' apartments; through workroom, scullery and stable; out to the last and least and meanest little yard; narrow and dark, stone-paved, stone-walled, shadowed by caves of barns; there, huddled in a barrel, they pointed out a man. They bowed to him, they called him master. They told me he was the owner of this vast estate. I could not believe it— but they stood bowing— and he ordered them away.

"What!" I cried. "You!— you are the owner— the master of all this wealth of beauty— this beauty of wealth! You own these miles of breezy upland and rich valley— still forests and bright lakes! You own these noble trees— those overflowing flowers— those glades of browsing deer! You own this palace— a joy to the eye and uplift to the soul! This majesty and splendor— this comfort, beauty, form, you own all this— and are living— here."

He regarded me superciliously, with a weary expression.

"Young man," he said, "you are a dreamer— a visionary— a Utopian!— an idealist! You should consider Facts, my young sir; fix your mind on Facts! The Fact is that I live in this Barrel."

It was a fact;— he did visibly live in the Barrel. It was also a fact that he owned that vast estate. And there was no lid on the Barrel.

* * * * *

Two Storks

Two storks were nesting. He was a young stork— and narrow-minded. Before he married he had consorted mainly with striplings of his own kind, and had given no thought to the ladies, either maid or matron. After he married his attention was concentrated upon his all-satisfying wife; upon that triumph of art, labor, and love— their nest, and upon those special creations — their children.

Deeply was he moved by the marvelous instincts and processes of motherhood. Love, reverence, intense admiration, rose in his heart for her of the well-built nest; her of the gleaming treasure of smooth eggs; her of the patient brooding breast, the warming wings, the downy wide-mouthed group of little ones.

Assiduously he labored to help her build the nest, to help her feed the young; proud of his impassioned activity in her and their behalf; devoutly he performed his share of the brooding, while she hunted in her turn. When he was on the wing he thought continually of her as one with the brood— his brood. When he was on the nest he thought all the more of her, who sat there so long, so lovingly, to such noble ends.

The happy days flew by, fair Spring— sweet Summer— gentle Autumn. The young ones grew larger and larger; it was more and more work to keep their lengthening, widening beaks shut in contentment.

Both parents flew far afield to feed them. Then the days grew shorter, the sky grayer, the wind colder; there was less hunting and small success. In his dreams he began to see sunshine, broad, burning sunshine day after day; skies of limitless blue; dark, deep, yet full of fire; and stretches of bright water, shallow, warm, fringed with tall reeds and rushes, teeming with fat frogs. They were in her dreams too, but he did not know that.

He stretched his wings and flew farther every day; but his wings were not satisfied. In his dreams came a sense of vast heights and boundless spaces of the earth streaming away beneath him; black water and white land, gray water and brown land, blue water and green land, all flowing backward from day to day, while the cold lessened and the warmth grew.

He felt the empty sparkling nights, stars far above, quivering, burning; stars far below, quivering more in the dark water; and felt his great wings wide, strong, all sufficient, carrying him on and on! This was in her dreams too, but he did not know that.

"It is time to Go!" he cried one day. "They are coming! It is upon us! Yes— I must Go! Goodbye my wife! Goodbye my children!" For the Passion of Wings was upon him.

She too was stirred to the heart. "Yes! It is time to Go! To Go!" she cried. "I am ready! Come!"

He was shocked; grieved; astonished. "Why, my Dear!" he said. "How preposterous! You cannot go on the Great Flight! Your wings are for brooding tender little ones! Your body is for the Wonder of the Gleaming Treasure!— not for days and nights of ceaseless soaring! You cannot go!"

She did not heed him. She spread her wide wings and swept and circled far and high above— as, in truth, she had been doing for many days, though he had not noticed it. She dropped to the ridge-pole beside him where he was still muttering objections. "Is it not glorious!" she cried. "Come! They are nearly ready!"

"You unnatural Mother!" he burst forth. "You have forgotten the Order of Nature! You have forgotten your Children! Your lovely precious tender helpless little ones!" And he wept— for his highest ideals were shattered. But the precious little ones stood in a row on the ridge-pole and flapped their strong young wings in high derision. They were as big as he was, nearly; for as a matter of fact he was but a young stork himself.

Then the air was beaten white with a thousand wings, it was like snow and silver and sea foam, there was a flashing whirlwind, a hurricane of wild joy and then the army of the sky spread wide in due array and streamed Southward. Full of remembered joy and more joyous hope, finding the high sunlight better than her dreams, she swept away to the far summer land; and her children, mad with the happiness of the first flight, swept beside her.

"But you are a Mother!" he panted, as he caught up with them.

"Yes!" she cried, joyously, "but I was a stork before I was a mother! and afterward!— and All the Time!"

And the storks were flying.

* * * * *

88

A Coincidence

"O that! It was a fortunate coincidence, wasn't it?" All things work together for good with those who love the Lord, you know, and Emma Ordway is the most outrageously Christian woman I ever knew. It did look that Autumn as if there was no way out of it, but things do happen, sometimes.

I dropped in rather late one afternoon to have a cup of tea with Emma, hoping against hope that Mirabella Vlack wouldn't be on hand; but she was, of course, and gobbling. There never was such a woman for candy and all manner of sweet stuff. I can remember her at school, with those large innocent eyes, and that wide mouth, eating Emma's nicest tidbits even then.

Emma loves sweets but she loves her friends better, and never gets anything for herself unless there is more than enough for everybody. She is very fond of a particular kind of fudge I make, has been fond of it for thirty years, and I love to make it for her once in a while, but after Mirabella came— I might as well have made it for her to begin with. I devised the idea of bringing it in separate boxes, one for each, but bless you! Mirabella kept hers in her room, and ate Emma's!

"O I've left mine up stairs!" she'd say; "Let me go up and get it;"— and of course Emma wouldn't hear of such a thing. Trust Emma!

I've loved that girl ever since she was a girl, in spite of her preternatural unselfishness. And I've always hated those Vlack girls, both of them, Mirabella the most. At least I think so when I'm with her. When I'm with Arabella I'm not so sure. She married a man named Sibthorpe, just rich.

They were both there that afternoon, the Vlack girls I mean, and disagreeing as usual. Arabella was lean and hard and rigorously well dressed, she meant to have her way in this world and generally got it. Mirabella was thick and soft. Her face was draped puffily upon its unseen bones, and of an unwholesome color because of indigestion. She was the type that suggests cushioned upholstery, whereas Arabella's construction was evident.

"You don't look well, Mirabella," said she.

"I am well," replied her sister, "Quite well I assure you."

Mirabella was at that time some kind of a holy thoughtist. She had tried every variety of doctor, keeping them only as long as they did not charge too much, and let her eat what she pleased; which necessitated frequent change.

Mrs. Montrose smiled diplomatically, remarking "What a comfort these wonderful new faiths are!" She was one of Emma's old friends, and was urging her to go out to California with them and spend the winter. She dilated on the heavenly beauty and sweetness of the place till it almost made my mouth water, and Emma!— she loved travel better than anything, and California was one of the few places she had not seen.

Then that Vlack girl began to perform. "Why don't you go, Emma?" she said. "I'm not able to travel myself," (she wouldn't admit she was pointedly left out), "but that's no reason you should miss such a delightful opportunity. I can be housekeeper for you in your absence." This proposition had been tried once. All Emma's old servants left, and she had to come back in the middle of her trip, and re-organize the household.

Thus Mirabella, looking saintly and cheerful. And Emma— I could have shaken her soundly where she sat— Emma smiled bravely at Mrs. Montrose and thanked her warmly; she'd love it above all things, but there were many reasons why she couldn't leave home that winter. And we both knew there was only one, a huge thing in petticoats sitting gobbling there.

One or two other old friends dropped in, but they didn't stay long; they never did any more, and hardly any men came now.

As I sat there drinking my pale tea I heard these people asking Emma why she didn't do this any more, and why she didn't come to that any more, and Emma just as dignified and nice as you please, telling all sorts of perforated paper fibs to explain and decline. One can't be perfect, and nobody could be as absolutely kind and gracious and universally beloved as Emma if she always told the plain truth.

I'd brought in my last protege that day, Dr. Lucy Barnes, a small quaint person, with more knowledge of her profession than her looks would indicate. She was a very wise little creature altogether. I had been studying chemistry with her, just for fun. You never know when yon may want to know a thing. It was fine to see Dr. Lucy put her finger on Mirabella's weakness.

There that great cuckoo sat and discoursed on the symptoms she used to have, and would have now if it wasn't for "science"; and there I sat and watched Emma, and I declare she seemed to age visibly before my eyes.

Was I to keep quiet and let one of the nicest women that ever breathed be worn into her grave by that— Incubus? Even if she hadn't been a friend of mine, even if she hadn't been too good for this world, it would have been a shame. As it was the outrage cried to heaven;— and nobody could do anything.

Here was Emma, a widow, and in her own house; you couldn't coerce her. And she could afford it, as far as money went, you couldn't interfere that way. She had been so happy! She'd got over being a widow— I mean got used to it, and was finding her own feet. Her children were all married and reasonably happy, except the youngest, who was unreasonably happy; but time would make that all right. Emma really began to enjoy life. Her health was good; she'd kept her looks wonderfully; and all the vivid interests of her girlhood cropped up again.

She began to study things; to go to lectures and courses of lectures; to travel every year to a new place; to see her old friends and make new ones. She never liked to keep house, but Emma was so idiotically unselfish that she never would enjoy herself as long as there was anybody at home to give up to. And then came Mirabella Vlack.

She came for a visit, at least she called one day with her air of saintly patience, and a miserable story of her loneliness and unhappiness, and how she couldn't bear to be dependent on Arabella— Arabella was so unsympathetic!— and that misguided Emma invited her to visit her for awhile. That was five years ago. Five years! And here she sat, gobbling, forty pounds fatter and the soul of amiability, while Emma grew old.

Of course we all remonstrated— after it was too late. Emma had a right to her own visitors— nobody ever dreamed that the thing was permanent, and nobody could break down that adamantine wall of Christian virtue she suffered behind, not owning that she suffered. It was a problem. But I love problems, human problems, better even than problems in chemistry, and they are fascinating enough.

First I tried Arabella. She said she regretted that poor Mirabella would not come to her loving arms. You see Mirabella had tried them, for about a year after her husband died, and preferred Emma's.

"It really doesn't look well," said Arabella. "Here am I alone in these great halls, and there is my only sister preferring to live with a comparative stranger! Her duty is to live with me, where I can take care of her."

Not much progress here. Mirabella did not want to be taken care of by a fault-finding older sister— not while Emma was in reach. It paid, too. Her insurance money kept her in clothes, and she could save a good deal, having no living expenses. As long as she preferred living with Emma Ordway, and Emma let her— what could anybody do?

It was getting well along in November, miserable weather. Emma had a cough that hung on for weeks and weeks, she couldn't seem to gather herself together and throw it off, and Mirabella all the time assuring her that she had no cough at all! Certain things began to seem very clear to me. One was the duty of a sister, of two sisters. One was the need of a change of climate for my Emma. One was that ever opening field of human possibilities which it has been the increasing joy of my lifetime to study.

I carried two boxes of my delectable fudge to those ladies quite regularly, a plain white one for Emma, a pretty colored one for the Incubus.

"Are you sure it is good for you?" I asked Mirabella; "I love to make it and have it appreciated, but does your Doctor think it is good for you?"

Strong in her latest faith she proudly declared she could eat anything. She could— visibly. So she took me up short on this point, and ate several to demonstrate immunity— out of Emma's box. Nevertheless, in spite of all demonstration she seemed to grow somewhat— queasy— shall we say?— and drove poor Emma almost to tears trying to please her in the matter of meals.

Then I began to take them both out to ride in my motor, and to call quite frequently on Arabella; they couldn't well help it, you see, when I stopped the car and hopped out. "Mrs. Sibthorpe's sister" I'd always say to the butler or maid, and she'd always act as if she owned the house— that is if Arabella was out.

Then I had a good talk with Emma's old doctor, and he quite frightened her.

"You ought to close up the house," he said, "and spend the winter in a warm climate. You need complete rest and change, for a long time, a year at least," he told her. I urged her to go.

"Do make a change," I begged. "Here's Mrs. Sibthorpe perfectly willing to keep Mirabella— she'd be just as well off there; and you do really need a rest."

Emma smiled that saintly smile of hers, and said, "Of course, if Mirabella would go to her sister's awhile I could leave? But I can't ask her to go."

I could. I did. I put it to her fair and square,— the state of Emma's health, her real need to break up housekeeping, and how Arabella was just waiting for her to come there. But what's the use of talking to that kind? Emma wasn't sick, couldn't be sick, nobody could. At that very moment she paused suddenly, laid a fat hand on a fat side with an expression that certainly looked like pain; but she changed it for one of lofty and determined faith, and seemed to feel better. It made her cross though, as near it as she ever gets. She'd have been rude I think, but she likes my motor, to say nothing of my fudge.

I took them both out to ride that very afternoon, and Dr. Lucy with us. Emma, foolish thing, insisted on sitting with the driver, and Mirabella made for her pet corner at once. I put Dr. Lucy in the middle, and encouraged Mirabella in her favorite backsliding, the discussion of her symptoms— the symptoms she used to have — or would have now if she gave way to "error."

Dr. Lucy was ingeniously sympathetic. She made no pretense of taking up the new view, but was perfectly polite about it.

"Judging from what you tell me", she said, "and from my own point of view, I should say that you had a quite serious digestive trouble; that you had a good deal of pain now and then; and were quite likely to have a sudden and perhaps serious attack. But that is all nonsense to you I suppose."

"Of course it is!" said Mirabella, turning a shade paler.

We were running smoothly down the to avenue where Arabella lived. "Here's something to cheer you up," I said, producing my two boxes of fudge. One I passed around in front to Emma; she couldn't share it with us. The other I gave Mirabella. She fell upon it at once; perfunctorily offering some to Dr. Lucy, who declined; and to me. I took one for politeness's sake, and casually put it in my pocket. We had just about reached Mrs. Sibthorpe's gate when Mirabella gave in.

"Oh I have such a terrible pain!" said she. "Oh Dr. Lucy! What shall I do?"

"Shall I take you down to your healer?" I suggested; but Mirabella was feeling very badly indeed.

"I think I'd better go in here a moment," she said; and in five minutes we had her in bed in what used to be her room. Dr. Lucy seemed averse to prescribe.

"I have no right to interfere with your faith, Mrs. Vlack," she said. "I have medicines which I think would relieve you, but you do not believe in them. I think you should summon your— practitioner, at once."

"Oh Dr. Lucy!" gasped poor Mirabella, whose aspect was that of a small boy in an August orchard. "Don't leave me! Oh do something for me quick!"

"Will you do just what I say?"

"I will! I will; I'll do anything!" said Mirabella, curling up in as small a heap as was possible to her proportions, and Dr. Lucy took the case. We waited in the big bald parlors till she came down to tell us what was wrong. Emma seemed very anxious, but then Emma is a preternatural saint.

Arabella came home and made a great todo. "So fortunate that she was near my door!" she said. "Oh my poor sister! I am so glad she has a real doctor!"

The real doctor came down after a while. "She is practically out of pain," she said, "and resting quietly. But she is extremely weak, and ought not to be moved for a long time."

"She shall not be!" said Arabella fervently. "My own sister! I am so thankful she came to me in her hour of need!"

I took Emma away. "Let's pick up Mrs. Montrose," I said. "She's tired out with packing— the air will do her good."

She was glad to come. We all sat back comfortably in the big seat and had a fine ride; and then Mrs. Montrose had us both come in and take dinner with her. Emma ate better than I'd seen her in months, and before she went home it was settled that she leave with Mrs. Montrose on Tuesday.

Dear Emma! She was as pleased as a child. I ran about with her, doing a little shopping. "Don't bother with anything," I said, "You can get things out there. Maybe you'll go on to Japan next spring with the James's."

"If we could sell the house I would!" said Emma. She brisked and sparkled— the years fell off from her— she started off looking fairly girlish in her hope and enthusiasm.

I drew a long sigh of relief.

Mr. MacAvelly has some real estate interests. The house was sold before Mirabella was out of bed.

* * * * *

While The King Slept

He was a young king, but an old subject, for he had been born and raised a subject, and became a king quite late in life, and unexpectedly.

When he was a subject he had admired and envied kings, and had often said to himself "If I were a king I would do this— and this." And now that he was a king he did those things. But the things he did were those which came from the envy of subjects, not from the conscience of kings.

He lived in freedom and ease and pleasure, for he did not know that kings worked; much less how their work should be done. And whatever displeased him he made laws against, that it should not be done; and whatever pleased him he made laws for, that it should be done— for he thought kings need but to say the word and their will was accomplished.

Then when the things were not done, when his laws were broken and disregarded and made naught of, he did nothing; for he had not the pride of kings, and knew only the outer showing of their power. And in his court and his country there flourished *sly thieves* and *gay wantons* and *bold robbers*; also poisoners and *parasites* and *impostors* of every degree.

And when he was very angry he slew one and another; but there were many of them, springing like toadstools, so that his land became a scorn to other kings. He was sensitive and angry when the old kings of the old kingdoms criticized his new kingdom.

"They are envious of my new kingdom;" he said; for he thought his kingdom was new, because he was new to it.

Then arose friends and counselors, many and more, and they gave him criticism and suggestion, blame, advice, and special instructions. Some he denied and some he neglected and some he laughed at and some he would not hear.

And when the *sly thieves* and *gay wantons* and *bold robbers* and *poisoners* and *parasites* and *imposters* of every degree waxed fat before his eyes, and made gorgeous processions with banners before him, he said, "How prosperous my country is!"

Then his friends and counselors showed him the prisons—overflowing; and the hospitals— overflowing; and the asylums—overflowing; and the schools— with not enough room for the children; and the churches— with not enough children for the room; and the *crime mill*, into which babies were poured by the hundreds every day, and out of which criminals were poured by the hundreds every day; and the *disease garden*, where we raise all diseases and distribute them gratis.

And he said "I am tired of looking at these things, and tired of hearing about them. Why do you forever set before me that which is unpleasant?"

And they said "Because you are the king. If you choose you can turn the empty churches into free schools, teaching Heaven Building. You can gradually empty the hospitals and asylums and prisons, and destroy the *crime mill*, and obliterate the *disease garden*."

"You are dreamers and mad enthusiasts. These things are the order of nature and cannot be stopped. It was always so." the king said, for the king had been a subject all his life, and was used to submission; he knew not the work of kings, nor how to do it.

And the false counselors and the false friends and all the lying servants who stole from the kitchens and the chambers answered falsely when he asked them, and said, "These evils are the order of nature. Your kingdom is very prosperous."

And the *sly thieves* and the *gay wantons* and the *bold robbers* and the *parasites* and *poisoners* and *impostors* of every degree hung like leeches on the kingdom and bled it at every pore.

But the king was weary and slept.

Then the friends and counselors went to the Queen, and called on her to learn Queen's work, and do it; for the King slept.

"It is King's work," she said, and strove to waken him with tales of want and sorrow in his kingdom. But he sent her away, saying "I will sleep."

"It is Queen's work also," they said to her; and though she had been a subject with her husband, she was more by nature a Queen. So she fell to and learned Queen's work, and did it.

She had no patience with the *gay wantons* and *sly thieves* and *bold robbers*; and the *poisoners* and the *parasites* and the *impostors* of every degree were a horror to her.

The false friends she saw through, and the lying servants she disbelieved.

Since the king would not, she would; and when at last he woke, behold, the throne a double one, and the kingdom smiled and rejoiced from sea to sea.

* * * * *

Charlotte Gilman

The Cottagette

"Why not?" said Mr. Mathews "It is far too small for a house, too pretty for a hut, too unusual for a cottage."

"Cottagette, by all means," said Lois, seating herself on a porch chair.

"But it is larger than it looks, Mr. Mathews. How do you like it, Malda?"

I was delighted with it. More than delighted. Here this tiny shell of fresh unpainted wood peeped out from under the trees, the only house in sight except the distant white specks on far off farms, and the little wandering village in the river-threaded valley. It sat right on the turf,— no road, no path even, and the dark woods shadowed the back windows.

"How about meals?" asked Lois.

"Not two minutes walk," he assured her, and showed us a little furtive path between the trees to the place where meals were furnished. We discussed and examined and exclaimed, Lois holding her pongee skirts close about her— she needn't have been so careful, there wasn't a speck of dust,— and we decided to take it.

Never did I know the real joy and peace of living, before that blessed summer at "High Court." It was a mountain place, easy enough to get to, but strangely big and still and far away when you were there. The working basis of the establishment was an eccentric woman named Caswell, a sort of musical enthusiast, who had a summer school of music and the "higher things." Malicious persons, not able to obtain accommodations there, called the place "High C."

I liked the music very well, and kept my thoughts to myself, both high and low, but "The Cottagette" I loved unreservedly. It was so little and new and clean, smelling only of its fresh-planed boards— they hadn't even stained it.

There was one big room and two little ones in the tiny thing, though from the outside you wouldn't have believed it, it looked so small; but small as it was it harbored a miracle— a real bathroom with water piped from mountain springs.

Our windows opened into the green shadiness, the soft brownness, the bird-inhabited quiet flower-starred woods. But in front we looked across whole counties— over a far-off river-into another state. Off and down and away— it was like sitting on the roof of something— something very big.

The grass swept up to the door-step, to the walls— only it wasn't just grass of course, but such a procession of flowers as I had never imagined could grow in one place. You had to go quite a way through the meadow, wearing your own narrow faintly marked streak in the grass, to reach the town-connecting road below. But in the woods was a little path, clear and wide, by which we went to meals. For we ate with the highly thoughtful musicians, and highly musical thinkers, in their central boarding-house nearby.

They didn't call it a boarding-house, which is neither high nor musical; they called it "The Calceolaria." There was plenty of that growing about, and I didn't mind what they called it so long as the food was good— which it was, and the prices reasonable— which they were.

The people were extremely interesting— some of them at least; and all of them were better than the average of summer boarders. But if there hadn't been any interesting ones it didn't matter while Ford Mathews was there. He was a newspaper man, or rather an ex-newspaper man, then becoming a writer for magazines, with books ahead.

He had friends at High Court— he liked music— he liked the place— and he liked us. Lois liked him too, as was quite natural. I'm sure I did. He used to come up evenings and sit on the porch and talk. He came daytimes and went on long walks with us. He established his workshop in a most attractive little cave not far beyond us— the country there is full of rocky ledges and hollows — and sometimes asked us over to an afternoon tea, made on a gypsy fire.

Lois was a good deal older than I, but not really old at all, and she didn't look her thirty-five by ten years. I never blamed her for not mentioning it, and I wouldn't have done so, myself, on any account. But I felt that together we made a safe and reasonable household. She played beautifully, and there was a piano in our big room. There were pianos in several other little cottages about — but too far off for any jar of sound.

When the wind was right we caught little wafts of music now and then; but mostly it was still— blessedly still, about us. And yet that Calceolaria was only two minutes off— and with raincoats and rubbers we never minded going to it.

We saw a good deal of Ford and I got interested in him, I couldn't help it. He was big. Not extra big in pounds and inches, but a man with big view and a grip— with purpose and real power. He was going to do things. I thought he was doing them now, but he didn't— this was all like cutting steps in the ice-wall, he said. It had to be done, but the road was long ahead. And he took an interest in my work too, which is unusual for a literary man.

Mine wasn't much. I did embroidery and made designs. It is such pretty work! I like to draw from flowers and leaves and things about me; conventionalize them sometimes, and sometimes paint them just as they are,— in soft silk stitches.

All about up here were the lovely small things I needed; and not only these, but the lovely big things that make one feel so strong and able to do beautiful work. Here was the friend I lived so happily with, and all this fairy land of sun and shadow, the free immensity of our view, and the dainty comfort of the Cottagette. We never had to think of ordinary things till the soft musical thrill of the Japanese gong stole through the trees, and we trotted off to the Calceolaria.

I think Lois knew before I did. We were old friends and trusted each other, and she had experience too. "Malda," she said, "let us face this thing and be rational." It was a strange thing that Lois should be so rational and yet so musical— but she was, and that was one reason I liked her so much.

"You are beginning to love Ford Mathews— do you know it?"

I said yes, I thought I was.

"Does he love you?"

That I couldn't say. "It is early yet," I told her. "He is a man, he is about thirty I believe, he has seen more of life and probably loved before— it may be nothing more than friendliness with him."

"Do you think it would be a good marriage?" she asked. We had often talked of love and marriage, and Lois had helped me to form my views— hers were very clear and strong.

"Why yes— if he loves me," I said. "He has told me quite a bit about his family, good western farming people, real Americans. He is strong and well— you can read clean living in his eyes and mouth." Ford's eyes were as clear as a girl's, the whites of them were clear.

Most men's eyes, when you look at them critically, are not like that. They may look at you very expressively, but when you look at them, just as features, they are not very nice.

I liked his looks, but I liked him better.

So I told her that as far as I knew it would be a good marriage — if it was one.

"How much do you love him?" she asked.

That I couldn't quite tell,— it was a good deal,— but I didn't think it would kill me to lose him.

"Do you love him enough to do something to win him— to really put yourself out somewhat for that purpose?"

"Why— yes— I think I do. If it was something I approved of. What do you mean?"

Then Lois unfolded her plan. She had been married,— unhappily married, in her youth; that was all over and done with years ago; she had told me about it long since; and she said she did not regret the pain and loss because it had given her experience. She had her maiden name again— and freedom. She was so fond of me she wanted to give me the benefit of her experience— without the pain.

"Men like music," said Lois; "they like sensible talk; they like beauty of course, and all that,—"

"Then they ought to like you!" I interrupted, and, as a matter of fact they did. I knew several who wanted to marry her, but she said "once was enough." I don't think they were "good marriages" though.

"Don't be foolish, child," said Lois, "this is serious. What they care for most after all is domesticity. Of course they'll fall in love with anything; but what they want to marry is a homemaker. Now we are living here in an idyllic sort of way, quite conducive to falling in love, but no temptation to marriage. If I were you— if I really loved this man and wished to marry him, I would make a home of this place."

"Make a home?— why it is a home. I never was so happy anywhere in my life. What on earth do you mean, Lois?"

"A person might be happy in a balloon, I suppose," she replied, "but it wouldn't be a home. He comes here and sits talking with us, and it's quiet and feminine and attractive— and then we hear that big gong at the Calceolaria, and off we go stopping through the wet woods— and the spell is broken. Now you can cook."

I could cook. I could cook excellently. My esteemed Mama had rigorously taught me every branch of what is now called "domestic science;" and I had no objection to the work, except that it prevented my doing anything else. And one's hands are not so nice when one cooks and washes dishes,— I need nice hands for my needlework. But if it was a question of pleasing Ford Mathews—

Lois went on calmly. "Miss Caswell would put on a kitchen for us in a minute, she said she would, you know, when we took the cottage. Plenty of people keep house up here,— we, can if we want to."

"But we don't want to," I said, "we never have wanted to. The very beauty of the place is that it never had any house-keeping about it. Still, as you say, it would be cozy on a wet night, we could have delicious little suppers, and have him stay—"

"He told me he had never known a home since he was eighteen," said Lois.

That was how we came to install a kitchen in the Cottagette. The men put it up in a few days, just a lean-to with a window, a sink and two doors.

I did the cooking. We had nice things, there is no denying that; good fresh milk and vegetables particularly, fruit is hard to get in the country, and meat too, still we managed nicely; the less you have the more you have to manage— it takes time and brains, that's all.

Lois likes to do housework, but it spoils her hands for practicing, so she can't; and I was perfectly willing to do it— it was all in the interest of my own heart. Ford certainly enjoyed it. He dropped in often, and ate things with undeniable relish. So I was pleased, though it did interfere with my work a good deal.

I always work best in the morning; but of course housework has to be done in the morning too; and it is astonishing how much work there is in the littlest kitchen. You go in for a minute, and you see this thing and that thing and the other thing to be done, and your minute is an hour before you know it.

When I was ready to sit down the freshness of the morning was gone somehow. Before, when I woke up, there was only the clean wood smell of the house, and then the blessed out-of-doors: now I always felt the call of the kitchen as soon as I woke. An oil stove will smell a little, either in or out of the house; and soap, and— well you know if you cook in a bedroom how it makes the room feel differently? Our house had been only bedroom and parlor before. We baked too— the baker's bread was really pretty poor, and Ford did enjoy my whole wheat, and brown, and especially hot rolls and gems. it was a pleasure to feed him, but it did heat up the house, and me. I never could work much— at my work— baking days.

Then, when I did get to work, the people would come with things,— milk or meat or vegetables, or children with berries; and what distressed me most was the wheel-marks on our meadow. They soon made quite a road— they had to of course, but I hated it— I lost that lovely sense of being on the last edge and looking over— we were just a bead on a string like other houses.

But it was quite true that I loved this man, and would do more than this to please him. We couldn't go off so freely on excursions as we used, either; when meals are to be prepared someone has to be there, and to take in things when they come.

Sometimes Lois stayed in, she always asked to, but mostly I did. I couldn't let her spoil her summer on my account. And Ford certainly liked it. He came so often that Lois said she thought it would look better if we had an older person with us; and that her mother could come if I wanted her, and she could help with the work of course. That seemed reasonable, and she came. I wasn't very fond of Lois's mother, Mrs. Fowler, but it did seem a little conspicuous, Mr. Mathews eating with us more than he did at the Calceolaria.

There were others of course, plenty of them dropping in, but I didn't encourage it much, it made so much more work. They would come in to supper, and then we would have musical evenings. They offered to help me wash dishes, some of them, but a new hand in the kitchen is not much help, I preferred to do it myself; then I knew where the dishes were. Ford never seemed to want to wipe dishes; though I often wished he would.

So Mrs. Fowler came. She and Lois had one room, they had to,— and she really did a lot of the work, she was a very practical old lady. Then the house began to be noisy. You hear another person in a kitchen more than you hear yourself, I think,— and the walls were only boards. She swept more than we did too. I don't think much sweeping is needed in a clean place like that; and she dusted all the time; which I know is unnecessary.

I still did most of the cooking, but I could get off more to draw, out-of-doors; and to walk. Ford was in and out continually, and, it seemed to me, was really coming nearer. What was one summer of interrupted work, of noise and dirt and smell and constant meditation on what to eat next, compared to a lifetime of love? Besides— if he married me— I should have to do it always, and might as well get used to it. Lois kept me contented, too, telling me nice things that Ford said about my cooking. "He does appreciate it so," she said.

One day he came around early and asked me to go up Hugh's Peak with him. It was a lovely climb and took all day.

I demurred a little, it was Monday, Mrs. Fowler thought it was cheaper to have a woman come and wash, and we did, but it certainly made more work.

"Never mind," he said, "what's washing day or ironing day or any of that old foolishness to us? This is walking day— that's what it is." It was really, cool and sweet and fresh,— it had rained in the night,— and brilliantly clear.

"Come along!" he said. "We can see as far as Patch Mountain I'm sure. There will never be a better day."

"Is anyone else going?" I asked.

"Not a soul. It's just us. Come."

I came gladly, only suggesting— "Wait, let me put up a lunch."

"I'll wait just long enough for you to put on knickers and a short skirt," said he. "The lunch is all in the basket on my back. I know how long it takes for you women to 'put up' sandwiches and things."

We were off in ten minutes, light-footed and happy, and the day was all that could be asked. He brought a perfect lunch, too, and had made it all himself. I confess it tasted better to me than my own cooking; but perhaps that was the climb.

When we were nearly down we stopped by a spring on a broad ledge, and supped, making tea as he liked to do out-of-doors. We saw the round sun setting at one end of a world view, and the round moon rising at the other; calmly shining each on each.

And then he asked me to be his wife.— We were very happy.

"But there's a condition!" said he all at once, sitting up straight and looking very fierce. "You mustn't cook!"

"What!" said I. "Mustn't cook?"

"No," said he, "you must give it up— for my sake."

I stared at him dumbly.

"Yes, I know all about it," he went on, "Lois told me. I've seen a good deal of Lois— since you've taken to cooking. And since I would talk about you, naturally I learned a lot. She told me how you were brought up, and how strong your domestic instincts were— but bless your artist soul dear girl, you have some others!" Then he smiled rather queerly and murmured, "surely in vain the net is spread in the sight of any bird. I've watched you, dear, all summer;" he went on, "it doesn't agree with you. Of course the things taste good— but so do my things! I'm a good cook myself. My father was a cook, for years— at good wages. I'm used to it you see. One summer when I was hard up I cooked for a living— and saved money instead of starving."

"O ho!" said I, "that accounts for the tea— and the lunch!"

"And lots of other things," said he. "But you haven't done half as much of your lovely work since you started this kitchen business, and— you'll forgive me, dear— it hasn't been as good. Your work is quite too good to lose; it is a beautiful and distinctive art, and I don't want you to let it go. What would you think of me if I gave up my hard long years of writing for the easy competence of a well-paid cook!"

I was still too happy to think very clearly. I just sat and looked at him. "But you want to marry me?" I said.

"I want to marry you, Malda,— because I love you— because you are young and strong and beautiful— because you are wild and sweet and— fragrant, and— elusive, like the wild flowers you love. Because you are so truly an artist in your special way, seeing beauty and giving it to others. I love you because of all this, because you are rational and high-minded and capable of friendship,— and in spite of your cooking!"

"But— how do you want to live?"

"As we did here— at first," he said. "There was peace, exquisite silence. There was beauty— nothing but beauty. There were the clean wood odors and flowers and fragrances and sweet wild wind. And there was you— your fair self, always delicately dressed, with white firm fingers sure of touch in delicate true work. I loved you then. When you took to cooking it jarred on me. I have been a cook, I tell you, and I know what it is. I hated it— to see my wood-flower in a kitchen. But Lois told me about how you were brought up to it and loved it— and I said to myself, 'I love this woman; I will wait and see if I love her even as a cook.' And I do, Darling: I withdraw the condition. I will love you always, even if you insist on being my cook for life!"

"O I don't insist!" I cried. "I don't want to cook— I want to draw! But I thought— Lois said— How she has misunderstood you!"

"It is not true, always, my dear," said he, "that the way to a man's heart is through his stomach; at least it's not the only way. Lois doesn't know everything, she is young yet! And perhaps for my sake you can give it up. Can you sweet?"

Could I? Could I? Was there ever a man like this?

* * * * *

An Offender

"Where's Harry?" was Mr. Gortlandt's first question.

"He's gone to the country, to mother. It was so hot this last day or two, I've sent him out, with Miss Colton. I'm going Saturday. Sit down."

"I miss him," said her visitor, "more than I thought I could. I've learned more in these seven years than I thought there was to know. Or in the last two perhaps, since I've found you again."

She looked at him with a little still smile, but there was a puzzled expression behind it, as of one whose mind was not made up. They sat in the wide window of a top floor apartment, awning-shaded. A fresh breeze blew in upon them, and the city dust blew in upon them also, lying sandy on the broad sill. She made little wavy lines in it with one finger.

"These windows ought to be shut tight, I suppose, and the blinds, and the curtains. Then we should be cleaner."

"As to furniture," he agreed, "but not as to our lungs."

"I don't know about that," she said; "we get plenty of air— but see what's in it."

"A city is a dirty place at best; but Mary— I didn't come to consider the ethics of the dust— how much longer must I wait?" he asked, after a little pause. "Isn't two years courting, re-courting— enough? Haven't I learned my lesson yet?"

"Some of it, I think," she admitted, "but not all."

"What more do you ask?" he pursued earnestly. "Can't we come to a definite understanding? You'll be chasing off again in a few days; it's blessed luck that brought you to town just now, and that I happened to be here too."

"I don't how about the luck," said she. "It was business that brought me. I never was in town before when it was so hot."

"Why don't you go to a hotel? This apartment is right under the roof, gets the sun all day."

"It gets the breeze too, and sunlight is good. No, I'm better off in the apartment, with Harry. It was very convenient of the Grants to be away, and let me have it."

"How does Hal stand the weather?"

"Pretty well. But he was getting rather fretful, so I sent him off two hours ago. I do hope he won't run away from Miss Colton again. She's as nervous as I am about him."

"Don't you think he is fond of me?" asked the man. "I've got to catch up, you see. He can't help being mine— half mine," he hastily added, seeing a hint of denial in her look.

"Why yes, he seems fond of you, he is fond of you," she conceded. "I hope he always will be, and I believe you are beginning to love him."

"A pretty strong beginning, Mary," said the man. "Of course I don't pretend to have cared much at first, but now!— why he's so handsome, and quick, and such a good little duffer; and so affectionate! When he gives a jump and gets his arms around my neck and his legs around my waist and 'hugs me all over' as he calls it, I almost feel as if I was a mother! I can't say more than that, can I?"

"No, you certainly can't say more than that. I believe you, I'm not questioning," for he looked up sharply at her tone.

"I've never had much to do with children, you see," he went on slowly, "no little brothers or sisters, and then only— What astonishes me is how good they feel in your arms! The little fellow's body is so firm and sinewy— he wriggles like a fish— a big fish that you're trying to hold with both hands."

The mother smiled tenderly. She knew the feel of the little body so well! From the soft pink helplessness, the little head falling so naturally into the hollow of the arm or neck, the fumbling little hands; then the gradual gain in size and strength, till now she held that eager bounding little body, almost strong enough to get away from her— but not wanting to. He still loved to nestle up to "Muzz," and was but newly and partially won by this unaccustomed father.

"It's seven years Mary! That makes a man all over, they say. I'm sure it has made me over. I'm an older man— and I think, wiser. I've repented, I've outgrown my folly and seen the justice of my punishment. I don't blame you an atom for divorcing me— I think you did right, and I respect you for it. The biggest lesson I've learned is to love you! I can see— now— that I didn't before.

Her face hardened as she looked at him. "No, you didn't, Harry, you certainly didn't, nor the child— When I think of what I was when you married me! Of my proud health!—"

"You are not hurt!" he cried. "I don't mean that you haven't been hurt, I could kill myself when I think of how I made you suffer! But you are a finer woman now than you were then;

sweeter, stronger, wiser, and more beautiful. When I found you again in Liverpool two years ago it was a revelation. Now see— I don't even ask you to forgive me! I ask you to try me again and let me prove I can make it up to you and the boy!"

"It's not easy for me to forgive," she answered slowly— "I'm not of the forgiving nature. But there is a good deal of reason in your position. You were my husband, you are Hal's father, there's no escaping that."

"Perhaps, if you will let the rest of my life make up for that time of my Godforsaken meanness, you won't want to escape it, Mary! See— I have followed you about for two years. I accepted your terms, you did not promise me anything, but for the child's sake I might try once more, try only as one of many, to see if I could win you— again. And I love you now a hundred times better than I did when I married you!"

She fanned herself slowly with a large soft fan, and looked out across the flickering roofs. Below them lay the highly respectable street on which the house technically fronted, and the broad, crowded, roaring avenue which it really overlooked. The rattle of many drays and more delivery wagons rose up to them. An unusual jangle drowned his words just then and she smilingly interpreted "that's railroad iron— or girders, I can tell lots of them now. About four A. M. there is a string of huge milk wagons. But the worst is the cars. Hear that now— that's a flat wheel. How do you like it?"

"Mary— why do you bring up these cars again when I'm trying my best to show you my whole heart? Don't put things like that between us!"

"But they are between us, Henry, all the time. I hear you tell me you love me, and I don't doubt you do in a way; yes, as well as you can, very much indeed!— I know. But when it comes to this car question; when I talk to you of these juggernauts of yours; you are no more willing to do the right thing than you were when I first knew you."

Mr. Cortlandt's face hardened. He drew himself up from the eager position in which he had leaned forward, and evidently hesitated for a moment as to his words.

In spite of his love for this woman, who, as he justly said, was far more beautiful and winsome than the strong, angular, over-conscientious girl he had married, neglected and shamed, his feelings as a business man were strong within him.

"My dear— I am not personally responsible for the condition of these cars."

109

"You are President of the Company. You hold controlling shares of the stock. It was your vote that turned down the last improvement proposition."

He looked at her sharply. "I'm afraid someone has been prejudicing you against me Mary. You have more technical information than seems likely to have reached you by accident."

"It's not prejudice, but it is information; and Mr. Graham did tell me, if that's what you mean. But he cares. You know how hard the Settlement has worked to get the Company to make the streets safer for children— and you wouldn't do a thing."

Mr. Cortlandt hesitated. It would never do to pile business details on his suit for a love once lost and not yet regained.

"You make it hard for me Mary," he said. "Hard because it is difficult to explain large business questions to a— to anyone not accustomed to them. I cannot swing the affairs of a great corporation for personal ends, even to please you."

"That is not the point," she said quickly.

He flushed, and hastily substituted "Even to suit the noblest humanitarian feelings."

"Why not?" said she.

"Because that is not what street cars are run for," he pursued patiently. "But why must we talk of this? It seems to put you so far away. And you have given me no answer."

"I am sorry, but I am not ready yet."

"Is it Hugh Graham?" he demanded. The hot color leaped to her face, but she met his eyes steadily. "I am much interested in Mr. Graham," she said, "and in the noble work he is doing. I think I should really be happier with him than with you. We care for the same things, he calls out the best in me. But I have made no decision in his favor yet, nor in yours. Both of you have a certain appeal to my heart, both to my duty. With you the personal need, with him the hope of greater service. But— you are the father of the child, and that gives you a great claim. I have not decided."

The man looked relieved, and again drew his chair a little closer. The sharp clangor of the cars rose between them.

"You think I dragged in this car question," she said. "Really, I did it because it is that sort of thing which does most to keep us apart, and— I would like to remove it."

He leaned forward, playing with her big fan. "Let's remove it by all means!" he said.

She looked at his bent head, the dark hair growing somewhat thin on top, almost tenderly.

"If I could feel that you were truly on the right side, that you considered your work as social service, that you tried to run your cars to carry people— not to kill them!— If you could change your ground here I think— almost—" she stopped, smiling up at him, her fan in her lap, her firm delicate white hands eagerly clasped; then went on, "Don't you care at all for the lives lost every day in this great city— under your cars?"

"It cannot be helped, my dear. Our men are as careful as men can be. But these swarming children will play in the streets—"

"Where else can they play!" she interjected.

"And they get right in front of the cars. We are very sorry; we pay out thousands of dollars in damages: but it cannot be helped!"

She leaned back in her chair and her face grew cold.

"You speak as if you never heard of such things as fenders," she said.

"We have fenders!— almost every car—"

"Fenders! Do you call that piece of rat-trap a fender! Henry Cortlandt! We were in Liverpool when this subject first came up between us! They have fenders there that fend and no murder list!"

"Conditions are different there," said he with an enforced quiet. "Our pavement is different."

"Our children are not so different, are they?" she demanded. "Our mothers are made of the same stuff I suppose?"

"You speak as if I wanted to kill them! As if I liked to!"

"I thought at first it would hurt you as it did me," she said warmly. "I turned to you with real hope when we met in Liverpool. I was glad to think I knew you, and I had not been glad of that for long! I thought you would care, would do things."

Do what he would, his mouth set hard in its accustomed lines. "Those English fender are not practicable in this country, Mary. They have been tried."

"When? Where? By whom?" she threw at him. "I have read about it, and heard about it. I know there was an effort to get them adopted, and that they were refused. They cost more than this kind!" and she pointed disdainfully at the rattling bit of stub-toed slat-work in front of a passing car.

"Do you expect me to make a revolution in the street car system of America— to please you? Do you make it a condition? Perhaps I can accomplish it. Is it a bargain? Come—"

"No," she said slowly. "I'm not making bargains. I'm only wishing, as I have wished so often in years past— that you were a different kind of man—"

"What kind do you want me to be?"

"I want you to be— I wish you were— a man who cared to give perfect service to his country, in his business."

"Perhaps I can be yet. I can try. If I had you to help me, with your pure ideals, and the boy to keep my heart open for the children. I don't know much about these things, but I can learn. I can read, you can tell me what to read. We could study together. And in my position perhaps, I could really be of some service after all."

"Perhaps?" She watched him, the strong rather heavy face, the attractive smile, the eyes that interested and compelled. He was an able, masterful man. He surely loved her now. She could feel a power over him that her short miserable marriage had never given her; and her girlhood's attraction toward him reasserted itself.

A new noise rose about them, a dissonant mingled merry outcry, made into a level roaring sound by their height above the street.

"That's when the school up here lets out," she said. "We hear it every day. Just see the crowds of them!"

They leaned on the broad sill and watched the many-colored torrent of juveniles pouring past.

"One day it was different," she said. "A strange jarring shrillness in it, a peculiar sound. I looked out, and there was a fight going on; two boys tumbling about from one side of the street to the other, with a moving ring around them, a big crowd, all roaring in one key."

"You get a birds-eye view of life in these streets, don't you. Can you make out that little chap with the red hair down there?"

"No— we are both near-sighted, you know. I can't distinguish faces at this distance. Can you?"

"Not very clearly," he said. "But what a swarm they are!"

"Come away," said she, "I can't bear to look at them. So many children in that stony street, and those cars going up and down like roaring lions!" They drew back into the big sunny room, and she seated herself at the piano and turned over loose sheets of music. He watched her with a look of intensest admiration, she was so tall, so nobly formed, her soft rich gown flowed and followed as she walked, her white throat rose round and royal from broad smooth shoulders.

He was beside her; he took away the music, laid it out of reach, possessed himself of her hands.

"Give them back to me, Mary," he pleaded. "Come to me and help me to be a better man! Help me to be a good father. I need you!"

She looked at him almost pleadingly. His eyes, his voice, his hands,— they had their old-time charm for her. Yet he had only said "Perhaps"— and he might study, might learn. He asked her to help him, but he did not say "I will do this"— only "I may."

In the steady bright June sunshine, in the sifting dust of a city corner, in the dissonant, confused noise of the traffic below, they stood and looked at one another. His eyes brightened and deepened as he watched her changing color. Softly he drew her towards him. "Even if you do not love me now, you shall in time, you shall, my darling!" But she drew back from him with a frightened start, a look of terror.

"What has happened!" she cried. "It's so still!"

They both rushed to the window. The avenue immediately below them was as empty as midnight, and as silent. A great stillness widened and spread for the moment around one vacant motionless open car. Without passenger, driver, or conductor, it stood alone in the glaring space; and then, with a gasp of horror, they both saw. Right under their eyes, headed towards them, under the middle of the long car— a little child. He was quite still, lying face downward, dirty and tumbled, with helpless arms thrown wide, the great car holding him down like a mouse in a trap. Then people came rushing. She turned away, choking, her hands to her eyes.

"Oh!" she cried, "Oh! It's a child, a little child!"

"Steady, Mary, steady!" said he, "the child's dead. It's all over. He's quite dead. He never knew what hit him." But his own voice trembled. She made a mighty effort to control herself, and he tried to take her in his arms, to comfort her, but she sprang away from him with fierce energy.

"Very well!" she said. "You are right! The child is dead. We can not save him. No one can save him. Now come back— come here to the window— and see what follows. I want to see with my own eyes— and have you see— what is done when your cars commit murder! Child murder!" She held up her watch. "It's 12:10 now," she said.

She dragged him back to the window, and so evident was the struggle with which she controlled herself, so intense her agonized excitement, that he dared not leave her.

"Look!" she cried. "Look! See the crowd now!"

The first horrified rush away from the instrument of death was followed by the usual surging multitude. From every direction people gathered thickly in astonishing numbers, hustling and pushing about the quiet form upon the ground; held so flat between iron rails and iron wheels, so great a weight on so small a body!

The car, still empty, rose like an island from the pushing sea of heads. Men and women cried excited directions. They tried with swarming impotent hands to lift the huge mass of wood and iron off the small broken thing beneath it, so small that it did not raise the crushing weight from the ground. A whole line of excited men seized the side rail and strove to lift the car by it, lifting only the rail. The crowd grew momentously, women weeping, children struggling to see, men pushing each other, policemen's helmets rising among them. And still the great car stood there, on the body of the child.

"Is there no means of lifting these monsters?" she demanded. "After they have done it, can't they even get off."

He moistened his lips to answer. "There is a jacking crew," he said. "They will be here soon."

"Soon!" she cried. "Soon! Couldn't these monsters use their own power to lift themselves somehow? not even that?"

He said nothing. More policemen came, and made a scant space around the little body, covering it with a dark cloth. The motorman was rescued from many would be avengers, and carried off under guard.

"Ten minutes," said she looking at her watch. "Ten minutes and it isn't even off him yet!" and she caught her breath in a great sob. Then she turned on the man at her side: "Suppose his mother is in that crowd! She may be! Their children go to this school, they live all about below here, she can't even get in to see! And if she could, if she knew it was her child, she can't get him out!" Her voice rose to a cry.

"Don't, Mary," said he, hoarsely. "It's— it's horrible! Don't make it worse!"

She kept her eyes on her watch-face, counting the minutes She looked down at the crowd shuddering, and said over and over, under breath, "A little child! A little soft child!"

It was twelve minutes and a half before the jacking crew drove up, with their tools. It was a long time yet before they did their work, and that crushed and soiled little body was borne to a near-by area grating and laid there, wrapped in its dingy shroud, and guarded by a policeman. It was a full half hour before the ambulance arrived to take it away. She drew back then and crouched sobbing by the sofa. "O the poor mother! God help his mother!"

He sat tense and white for a while; and when she grew quieter he spoke. "You were right, Mary. I— naturally, I never— visualized it! It is horrible! I am going to have those fenders on every car of the four systems!"

She said nothing. He spoke again.

"I hate to leave you feeling so, Dear. Must I go?"

She raised a face that was years older, but did not look at him. "You must go. And you must never come back. I cannot bear to see your face again!" And she turned from him, shuddering.

* * * * *

Charlotte Gilman

Mr. Grey

I thought I knew what trouble was when Jimmy went away. It was bad enough when he was clerking in Barstow and I only saw him once a week; but now he'd gone to sea. He said he'd never earn much as a clerk, and he hated it too. He'd saved every cent he could of his wages and taken a share in the Mary Jenks, and I shouldn't see him again for a year maybe,— maybe more. She was a sealer.

O dear! I'd have married him just as he was; but he said he couldn't keep me yet, and if they had luck he'd make 400% on his savings that voyage, and it was all for me. My blessed Jimmy!

He hadn't been gone but a bare fortnight when "unmerciful disaster followed fast and followed faster" on our poor heads. First father broke his arm. There was the doctor to pay, and all that plaster cast thing, and of course I had to do the milking and all the work. I didn't mind that a bit. We hadn't any horse then, to take care of, and Rosy, our cow, was a dear; gentle as a kitten, and sweet-breathed as a baby. But it put back all the farm work, of course; we couldn't hire, and there wasn't enough to go shares on. Mother was pretty wretched, and no wonder.

Then Rosy was stolen! That did seem the last straw. As long as Rosy was there and I could milk her, we shouldn't starve. Poor father! There he sat, with that plaster arm in the sling— the other one looking so discouraged and nerveless, and his head bowed on his breast; the hand hanging, the strong busy fingers laxly open.

"I'll go and look," he said, starting up, "where's my hat?"

"It's no use looking, father," said I, "the halter's gone, there are big footprints beside her hoof-marks out to the road, and then quite a stamped place, and then wagon wheels and her nice little clean tracks going off after the wagon. Plain stolen."

He sat down again and groaned.

"Thought I heard a wagon in the middle of the night," said mother, weakly. Her face was flushed, and her eyes ran over. "I can't sleep much you know. I ought to have spoken, but you need your sleep." I ran to her and kissed her.

"Now mother dear! Don't you fret over it,— please don't! We'll find Rosy. I'll get Mrs. Clark to phone for me at once."

"'Phone where?" said father. "It's no use phoning. Its those gypsies. And they got to town hours ago— and Rosy's beef by this time." He set his jaw hard; but there were tears in his eyes, too.

I was nearly distracted myself. "If only Jimmy were here," I said, "he'd find her!"

"I don't doubt he'd make a try," said father, "but it's too late."

I ran over to Mrs. Clark, and we phoned to the police in Barstow, and sure enough they found the hide and horns! It didn't do us any good. They arrested some gypsies, but couldn't prove anything; shut one of them up for vagrancy, too,— but that didn't do us any good, either. And if they'd proved it and convicted him it wouldn't have brought back Rosy,— or given us another cow.

Then mother got sick. It was pure discouragement as much as anything, I think, and she missed Rosy's milk,— she used to half live on it. After she was sick she missed it more, there were so few things she could eat,— and not many of those I could get for her.

O how I did miss Jimmy! If he'd been there he'd have helped me to see over it all. "Sho!" he'd have said. "It's hard lines, little girl, now; but bless you, a broken arm's only temporary; your father will be as good as ever soon. And your mother will get well; she's a strong woman. I never saw a stronger woman of her age. And as to the food— just claim you're 'no breakfast' people, and believe in fasting for your health!"

That's the way Jimmy met things, and I tried to say it all to myself, and keep my spirits up,— and theirs. But Jimmy was at sea.

Well, father couldn't work, it had to be his right arm, of course. And mother couldn't work either; she was just helpless and miserable, and the more she worried the sicker she got, and the sicker she got the more she worried. My patience! How I did work! No time to read, no time to study, no time to sew on any of the pretty white things I was gradually accumulating.

I got up before daylight, almost; kept the house as neat as I could, and got breakfast, such as it was. Father could dress himself after a fashion, and he could sit with mother when I was outside working in the garden. I began that garden just as an experiment, the day after father broke his arm. The outlay was only thirty cents for lettuce and radish seed, but it took a lot of work.

Then there was mother to do for, and father to cheer up (which was hardest of all), and dinner and supper to get,— and nothing to get them with, practically.

The doctor didn't push us any, but father hates a debt as he hates poison, and mother is a natural worrier. "She is killing herself with worry," the doctor said; and he had no anti-toxin for that, apparently.

And then, as if that wasn't enough, that Mr. Robert Grey Sr. took advantage of our misfortunes and began to make up to me again. I never liked the old man since I was a little girl. He was always picking me up and kissing me, when I didn't want to in the least. When I got older he'd pinch my checks, and offer me a nickle if I'd kiss him.

Mother liked him, for he stood high in the church, and was a charitable soul. Father liked him because he was successful— father always admired successful men;— and Mr. Grey got his money honestly, too, father said. He was a kind old soul. He offered to send me to college, and I was awfully tempted; but father couldn't bear a money obligation,— and I couldn't bear Mr. Grey.

There was a Robert Grey Jr., who was disagreeable enough; a thin, pimply, sanctimonious young fellow, with a class of girls in Sunday-school. He was sickly enough, but Mr. Robert Grey Sr. was worse. He sort of tottered and threw his feet about as he walked; and kind or not kind, I couldn't bear him. But he came around now all the time. He brought mother nice things to eat,— you can't refuse gifts to the sick,— and they were awfully nice; he has a first class cook. And he brought so much that there was enough for father too. We had to eat it to save it, you see,— but I hated every mouthful. I lived on our potatoes mostly, and they were poor enough— in June— and no milk to go with them.

He came every day, bringing his basket of delicacies for mother, and he'd chat awhile with her— she liked it; and he'd sit and talk with father— he liked it; and then he'd hang around me — and I had to be civil to him! But I did not like it a bit. I couldn't bear the old man with his thin gray whiskers, and his watery gray eyes, and his big pink mouth— color of an old hollyhock. But he came and came, and nobody could fail to see what he wanted; but O dear me! How I wished for Jimmy. My big, strong, brisk boy, with the jolly laugh and the funny little swears that he invented himself!

I watched the shipping news, and waited and hoped; he might come back any time now, if they'd had luck. But he didn't come. Mr. Robert Grey Sr. was there every day— and Jimmy didn't come. I tried not to cry. I needed all my strength and courage to keep some heart in father and mother, and I tried always to remember what Jimmy would have said; how he'd have faced it.

"Don't be fazed by anything," he used to say. "Everything goes by— give it time. Don't holler! Don't give a jam!" (People always looked so surprised when Jimmy said "Jam!") "Just hang on and do the square thing. You're not responsible for other people's sorrows. Hold up your own end."

Jimmy was splendid! He used to read to me about an old philosopher called Euripides, and I got to appreciate him too. But when the papers were full of "Storms at sea"—" Terrible weather in the north"— "Gales"— "High winds"— "Losses in shipping"— it did seem as if I couldn't bear it. Then at last it came, in a terrible list of wrecks. The Mary Jenks— lost, with all on board. O what was the use of living! What did anything matter! Why couldn't I die! Why couldn't I die! But I didn't. My health was as good as ever; I could even sleep when I wasn't crying.

Working hard out of doors and not eating very much makes you sleep I guess, heart or no heart. And I had to keep on working; my lettuce was up and coming on finely, rows upon rows of it, just as I had planted it, two days apart. And the radishes too, they were eatable, and we tried them. But father laughed grimly at my small garden. "A lot of good that will do us, child!" he said. "O Jenny— there's more than that you can do for your poor mother! I know you feel badly, and ordinarily I wouldn't say a word, but you see how it is."

I saw how it was well enough, but it seemed to me too horrible to think of. To thrust that tottering old philanthropist right into my poor bleeding heart! I couldn't bear it. Mother never said a word. But she looked. She'd lie there with her big hollow eyes following me around the room; and when I came to do anything for her she'd look in my face so! It was more effective than all father's talks. For father had made up his mind now, and urged me all the time.

"We might as well face the facts, Jenny," he said. "James Young is gone, and I'm sorry; and you are naturally broken-hearted. But even if you were a widow I'd say the same thing. Here is this man who has been good to you since you were a child; he will treat you well, you'll have a home, you'll be provided for when he dies. I know you're not in love with him. I don't expect it. He don't either. He has spoken to me. He don't expect miracles. Here we are, absolutely living on his food! It— it is terrible to me, Jennie! But I couldn't refuse, for your mother's sake. Now if I could pocket my pride for her sake, can't you pocket your grief? You can't bring back the dead."

"O father, don't!" I said. "How can you talk so! O Jimmy! Jimmy!— If you were here!"

"He isn't here— he never will be!" said father steadily. "But your mother is here, and sick. Mr. Grey wants to send her to a sanitarium— 'as a friend.' I can't let him do that,— it would cost hundreds of dollars. But— as a son-in-law I could."

Mother didn't say a thing— dear mother. But she looked at me. They made me feel like a brute, between them; at least father did. He kept right on talking.

"Mr. Grey is a good man," he said, "an unusually good man. If he was a bad man I'd never say a word."

"He was when he was young, old Miss Green says," I answered.

"I am ashamed of you, Jennie," said father, "to listen to such scandalous gossip! How— how unmaidenly of you! I dare say he was a little wild,— forty years ago. Most young fellows are, and he was rich and handsome. But he has been a shining light in this community for forty years.— A good husband— a good father."

"What did his wife die of?" I asked suddenly.

"An operation,— but he did everything for her. She had the best doctors and nurses. She was a good deal of an invalid, I believe, after Robert Jr. was born."

"He's not much!" said I.

"No, Robert Jr. has been a great disappointment to his father —the great disappointment of his life, I may say; though he was very fond of his wife. But he won't trouble you any, Jenny; his father is going to send him to Europe for a long time— for his health. Now Jenny, all this is ancient history. Here is a good kind man who loves you dearly, and wants to marry you at once. If you do it you may save your mother's life,— and set me on my feet again for what remains of mine. I never said a word while you were engaged to Jimmy Young, but now it's a plain duty."

That night Mr. Grey Sr. came as usual. He had sent round his car and got mother to take a ride that afternoon. It did her good, too. And when he came father went out and sat with her, and left me to him:— and he asked me to marry him. He told me all the things he'd do for me— for mother— for father. He said he shouldn't live very long anyway, and then I could be my own mistress, with plenty of money. And I couldn't say a word, yes or no. I sat there, playing with the edge of the lamp-mat— and thinking of Jimmy. And then Mr. Robert Grey Sr. made a mistake. He got a hold of my hand and fingered it. He came and took me in his arms— and kissed my mouth.

I jerked away from him— he almost fell over. "No! O NO!" I cried. "I can't do it Mr. Grey. I simply can't!"

He turned the color of ashes.

"Why not?" he said.

"Because it isn't decent," said I firmly. "I can't bear to have you touch me— never could. I will be a servant to you— I will work for you— nurse you— but to be your wife!— I'm sorry Mr. Grey, but I can't do it."

I ran upstairs, and cried and cried; and I had reason to cry, for father was a living thundercloud after that, and mother was worse; and they wouldn't take any more of Mr. Grey's kindnesses, either of them.

My lettuce and radishes kept us alive until the potatoes were ripe. I sold them, fresh every day. Walked three miles with a big basket full every morning, to one of the summer hotels. It was awfully heavy, especially when it rained. They didn't pay much, but it kept us— a dollar a day, sometimes more.

Father got better in course of time, of course, and went to work on the farm in a discouraged sort of way. But mother was worse, if anything. She never blamed me— never said a word; but her eyes were a living reproach.

"Mother, dear," I begged her, "do forgive me! I'll work till I drop, for you; I'll deny myself everything: I'll do most anything that's decent and honest. But to marry a man you don't love is not honest; and to marry an old invalid like that—it's not decent."

She just sighed— didn't say anything.

"Cheer up mother, do! Father's almost well; we can get through this year somehow. Next year I can make enough to buy a cow, really."

But it wasn't more than a month from that time, I was sitting on the door stone at twilight— thinking of Jimmy, of course— and — there was Jimmy. I thought it was his ghost; but if it was it was a very warm-blooded one.

As to old Mr. Robert Grey, Sr., he persuaded little Grace Salters to marry him; a pretty, foolish, plump little thing; and if you'll believe it, she died within a year— she and her baby with her. Well. If ever anybody was glad I was. I don't mean glad she was dead, poor girl; but glad I didn't marry him, and did marry Jimmy.

* * * * *

A Word In Season

"Children pick up words like pigeons peas, And utter them again as God shall please." When Grandma came to the breakfast table with her sour little smile and her peremptory "Good morning," every one said "good morning" as politely and pleasantly as they could, but they didn't say very much else. They attempted bravely.

"A fine morning, Mother," Papa observed, but she only answered "Too cold."

"Did you sleep well, Mother?" ventured Mama; and the reply to that was, "No, I never do!"

Then Uncle John tried— he always tried once.

"Have you heard of our new machine, Mrs. Grey? We've got one now that will catch anything in a room— don't have to talk right into it."

Mrs. Grey looked at him coldly. "I do not take the least interest in your talking machines, Henry, as I have told you before." She had, many times before, but Uncle Henry never could learn the astonishing fact. He was more interested in his machines than he was in his business, by far; and spent all his spare time in tinkering with them.

"I think they are wonderful," said little Josie.

"You're my only friend, Kid! I believe you understand them almost as well is I do," her Uncle answered gaily; and finished his breakfast as quickly as possible. So did everybody. It was not appetizing to have Grandma say "How you do dawdle over your meals, Louise!"

Little Josephine slipped down from her chair, with a whispered "Excuse me Mama!" and whisked into her play room.

"How you do spoil that child!" said Grandma, and Mama closed her lips tight and looked at her husband.

"Now Mother, don't you fret about Josie," said he. "She's a good little girl and quiet as a mouse."

"Anything I can do for you downtown, Mother?"

"No thank you Joseph. I'll go to my room and be out of Louise's way."

"You're not in my way at all, Mother— won't you sit down stairs?" Young Mrs. Grey made a brave effort to speak cordially, but old Mrs. Grey only looked injured, and said "No thank you, Louise," as she went upstairs.

Dr. Grey looked at his wife. She met his eyes steadily, cheerfully. "I think Mother's looking better, don't you dear?" she said.

"There's nothing at all the matter with my mother— except—" he shut his mouth hard. "There are things I cannot say, Louise," he continued, "but others I can. Namely; that for sweetness and patience and gentleness you— you beat the Dutch! And I do appreciate it. One can't turn one's Mother out of the house, but I do resent her having another doctor!"

"I'd love your Mother, Joseph, if— if she was a thousand times worse!" his wife answered; and he kissed her with grateful love.

Sarah came in to clear the table, and Ellen stood in the pantry door to chat with her. "Never in my life did I see any woman with the patience of her!" said Ellen, wiping her mouth on her apron.

"She has need of it," said Sarah. "Any Mother-in-law is a trial I've heard, but this one is the worst. Why she must need live with them I don't see— she has daughters of her own."

"It is the daughter's husbands won't put up with her," answered Ellen, "they having the say of course. This man's her son— and he has to keep her if she will stay."

"And she is as rich as a Jew!" Sarah went on. "And never spending a cent! And the Doctor working night and day!"—

Then Mama came in and this bit of conversation naturally came to an end. A busy, quiet, sweet little woman was Mama; and small Josie flew into her arms and cuddled there most happily.

"Mama Dearest," she said, "How long is it to Christmas? Can I get my mat done for Grandma? And do you think she'll like it?"

"Well, well dear— that's three questions! It's two weeks yet to Christmas; and I think you can if you work steadily; and I hope she'll like it."

"And Mama— can I have my party?"

"I'm afraid not, dearest. You see Grandma is old, and she hates a noise and confusion— and parties are expensive. I'm sorry, child. Can't you think of something else you want, that Mother can give you?"

"No," said the child, "I've wanted a party for three years, Mama! Grandma just spoils everything!"

"No, no, dear— you must always love Grandma because she is

dear Papa's mother; and because she is lonely and needs our love.

"We'll have a party some day, Dearest— don't feel badly. And we always have a good time together, don't we?" They did; but just now the child's heart was set on more social pleasures, and she went sadly back to her playroom to work on that mat for Grandma.

It was a busy day. Mama's married sister came to see her, and the child was sent out of the room. Two neighbors called, and waited, chatting, some time before Mama came down. Grandma's doctor— who was not Papa— called; and her lawyer too; and they had to wait some time for the old lady to dress as she thought fitting. But Grandma's doctor and lawyer were very old friends, and seemed to enjoy themselves.

The minister came also, not Grandma's minister, who was old and thin and severe and wore a long white beard; but Mama's minister, who was so vigorous and cheerful, and would lift Josephine way up over his head— as if she was ten years old. But Mama sent her out of the room this time, which was a pity.

To be sure Josephine had a little secret trail from her playroom door— behind several pieces of furniture— right up to the back of the sofa where people usually sat, but she was not often interested in their conversation. She was a quiet child, busy with her own plans and ideas; playing softly by herself, with much imaginary conversation. She set up her largest doll, a majestic personage known as "The Lady Isobel," and talked to her.

"Why is my Grandma so horrid? And why do I have to love her? How can you love people— if you don't, Lady Isobel? Other girls' Grandmas are nice. Nelly Elder's got a lovely Grandma! She lets Nelly have parties and everything. Maybe if Grandma likes my mat she'll— be pleasanter. Maybe she'll go somewhere else to live — sometime. Don't you think so, Lady Isobel?"

The Lady Isobel's reply, however, was not recorded.

Grandma pursued her pious way as usual, till an early bedtime relieved the family of her presence. Then Uncle Harry stopped puttering with his machines and came out to be sociable with his sister. If Papa was at home they would have a game of solo— if not, they played cribbage, or quiet. Uncle Harry was the life of the household— when Grandma wasn't around.

"Well, Lulu," he said cheerfully, "What's the prospect? Can Joe make it?"

"No," said Mama. "It's out of the question. He could arrange about his practice easily enough but it's the money for the trip. He'll have to send his paper to be read."

"It's a shame!" said the young man, "He ought to be there. He'd do those other doctors good. Why in the name of reason don't the old lady give him the money— she could, easy enough."

"Joe never will ask her for a cent," answered Mrs. Grey, "and it would never occur to her to give him one! Yet I think she loves him best of all her children."

"Huh! Love!" said Uncle Harry.

Grandma didn't sleep well at night. She complained of this circumstantially and at length. "Hour after hour I hear the clock strike," she said. "Hour after hour!"

Little Josephine had heard the clock strike hour after hour one terrible night when she had an earache. She was really sorry for Grandma.

"And nothing to take up my mind," said Grandma, as if her mind was a burden to her. But the night after this she had something to take up her mind. As a matter of fact it woke her up, as she had napped between the clock's strikings. At first she thought the servants were in her room— and realized with a start that they were speaking of her.

"Why she must live with them I don't see— she has daughters of her own—"

With the interest of an eavesdropper she lay still, listening, and heard no good of herself.

"How long is it to Christmas?" she heard her grandchild ask, and beg her mother for the "party"— still denied her.

"Grandma spoils everything!" said the clear childish voice, and the mother's gentle one urged love and patience. It was some time before the suddenly awakened old lady, in the dark, realized the source of these voices— and then she could not locate it.

"It's some joke of that young man's" she said grimly— but the joke went on. It was Mrs. Grey's sister now, condoling with her about this mother-in-law.

"Why do you have to put up with it Louise? Won't any of her daughters have her?"

"I'm afraid they don't want her," said Louise's gentle voice. "But Joe is her son, and of course he feels that his home is his mother's. I think he is quite right. She is old, and alone— she doesn't mean to be disagreeable."

"Well, she achieves it without effort, then! A more disagreeable old lady I never saw, Louise, and I'd like nothing better than to tell her so!"

The old lady was angry, but impressed. There is a fascination in learning how others see us, even if the lesson is unpleasant. She heard the two neighbors who talked together before Mama came down, and their talk was of her— and of how they pitied young Mrs. Grey. "If I was in her shoes," said the older of the two, "I'd pick up and travel! She's only sixty-five and sound as a nut."

"Has she money enough?" asked the other.

"My, yes! Money to burn! She has her annuity that her father left her, and a big insurance—and house rents. She must have all of three thousand a year."

"And doesn't she pay board here?"

"Pay board! Not she. She wouldn't pay anything so long as she has a relative to live on. She's saved all her life. But nobody will get any good of it till she's dead."

This talk stopped when their hostess entered, changing to more general themes; but the interest revived when men's voices took up the tale.

"Yes— wants her will made again. Always making and unmaking and remaking. Harmless amusement, I suppose."

"She wastes good money on both of us— and I tell her so. But one can't be expected to absolutely refuse a patient."

"Or a client!"

"No. I suppose not."

"She's not really ill then?"

"Bless you, Ruthven, I don't know a sounder old woman anywhere. All she needs is a change— and to think of something besides herself! I tell her that, too and she says I'm so eccentric."

"Why in all decency don't her son do her doctoring?"

"I suppose he's too frank— and not quite able to speak his mind. He's a fine fellow. That paper of his will be a great feature of our convention. Shame he can't go."

"Why can't he? Can't afford it?"

"That's just it. You see the old lady don't put up— not a cent— and he has all he can do to keep the boys in college." And their conversation stopped, and Grandma heard her own voice— inviting the doctor up to her room— and making another appointment for the lawyer. Then it was the young minister, a cheerful, brawny youth, whom she had once described as a "Godless upstart!"

He appeared to be comforting young Mrs. Grey, and commending her. "You are doing wonders," he said, as their voices came into hearing, "and not letting your right hand know it, either."

"You make far too much of it, Mr. Eagerson," the soft voice answered, "I am so happy in my children— my home— my husband. This is the only trouble— I do not complain."

"I know you don't complain, Mrs. Grey, but I want you to know that you're appreciated! 'It is better to dwell in a corner of the housetop, than with a woman in a wide house'— especially if she's your mother-in-law."

"I won't allow you to speak so— if you are my minister!" said young Mrs. Grey with spirit; and the talk changed to church matters, where the little lady offered to help with time and service, and regretted that she had no money to give. There was a silence, save for small confused noises of a day time household; distant sounds of doors and dishes; and then in a sad, confidential voice— "Why is Grandma so horrid? And why do I have to love her? How can you love people you don't, Lady Isobel?"

Grandma was really fond of quiet little Josephine, even if she did sometimes snub her as a matter of principle. She lay and listened to these strictly private remarks, and meditated upon them after they had ceased. It was a large dose, an omnibus dose, and took some time to assimilate; but the old lady had really a mind of her own, though much of it was uninhabited, and this generous burst of light set it to working. She said nothing to anyone, but seemed to use her eyes and ears with more attention than previously, and allowed her grand-daughter's small efforts toward affection with new receptiveness. She had one talk with her daughter-in-law which left that little woman wet-eyed and smiling with pleasure, though she could not tell about it— that was requisite. But the family in general heard nothing of any change of heart till breakfast time on Christmas morning. They sat enjoying that pleasant meal, in the usual respite before the old lady appeared, when Sarah came in with a bunch of notes and laid one at each plate, with an air of great importance.

"She said I was to leave them till you was all here— and here they are!" said Sarah, smiling mysteriously, "and that I was to say nothing— and I haven't!" And the red-cheeked girl folded her arms and waited— as interested as anybody.

Uncle Harry opened his first. "I bet it's a tract!" said he. But he blushed to the roots of his thick brown hair as he took out, not a tract, but a check.

"A Christmas present to my son-in-law-by-marriage; to be spent on the improvement of talking machines— if that is necessary!"

"Why bless her heart!" said he, "I call that pretty handsome, and I'll tell her so!"

Papa opened his. "For your Convention trip, dear son," said this one, "and for a new dress suit— and a new suit case, and a new overcoat— a nice one. With Mother's love." It was a large check, this one. Papa sat quite silent and looked at his wife. She went around the table and hugged him— she had to.

"You've got one, too, Louise," said he— and she opened it.

"For my dear daughter Louise; this— to be spent on other people; and this" (this was much bigger) "to be inexorably spent on herself— every cent of it! On her own special needs and pleasures— if she can think of any!" Louise was simply crying— and little Josephine ran to comfort her.

"Hold on Kiddie— you haven't opened yours," said Uncle Harry; and they all eagerly waited while the child carefully opened her envelope with a clean knife, and read out solemnly and slowly, "For my darling Grand-child Josephine, to be spent by herself, for herself, with Mama's advice and assistance; and in particular to provide for her party!" She turned over the stiff little piece of paper— hardly understanding.

"It's a check, dear," said Papa. "It's the same as money. Parties cost money, and Grandma has made you a Christmas present of your party." The little girl's eyes grew big with joy. "Can I?— Is there really— a party?"

"There is really a party— for my little daughter, this afternoon at four!"

"O where is Grandma!" cried the child— "I want to hug her!" They all rose up hurriedly, but Sarah came forward from her scant pretense of retirement, with another note for Dr. Grey. "I was to give you this last of all," she said, with an air of one fulfilling grave diplomatic responsibility.

"My dear ones," ran the note, "I have gathered from my family and friends, and from professional and spiritual advisers the idea that change is often beneficial. With this in mind I have given myself a Christmas present of a Cook's Tour around the world— and am gone. A Merry Christmas and a Happy New Year to you all!" She was gone. Sarah admitted complicity.

"Sure she would have no one know a thing— not a word!" said Sarah. "And she gave us something handsome to help her! And she's got that young widder Johnson for a companion— and they went off last night on the sleeper for New York!"

The gratitude of the family had to be spent in loving letters, and in great plans of what they would do to make Grandma happy when she came back.

No one felt more grateful than little loving Josephine, whose dearest wishes were all fulfilled. When she remembered it she went very quietly, when all were busy somewhere else, climbed up on the step ladder, and took down the forgotten phonograph from the top of the wardrobe.

"Dear Grandma!" she said. "I do hope she liked it!"

* * * * *

My Astonishing Dodo

She was twenty-six, and owned it cheerfully, the day I met her. This prejudiced me in her favor at once, for I prize honesty in women, and on this point it is unusual. She did not, it is true, share largely in my special artistic tastes, or, to any great extent, in my social circle; but she was a fine wholesome sweet woman, cheerful and strong, and I wished to make a friend of her.

I greatly prized my good friends among women, for I had conscientious views against marrying on a small salary. Later it appeared that she had other and different views, but she did not mention them then. Dorothea was her name. Her family called her Dora, her intimate friends, Dolly, but I called her Dodo, just between ourselves. A very good-looking girl was Dodo, though not showy; and in no way distinguished in dress, which rather annoyed me at first; for I have a great admiration for a well-gowned, well-groomed woman.

My ideas on matrimony were strongly colored by certain facts and figures given me by an old college friend of mine. He was a nice fellow, and his wife one of the loveliest girls of our set, though rather delicate. They lived very comfortably in a quiet way, with a few good books and pictures, and four little ones.

"It's a thousand dollars a year for the first year for each baby," he told me, "and five hundred a year afterward." I was astonished. I had no idea the little things cost so much.

"There's the trained nurse for your wife," he went on, "at $25 a week for four weeks; and then the trained nurse for your baby, at $15 a week for forty-eight weeks; that makes $820. Then the doctor's bills, the clothes and so on— with the certified milk— easily take up the rest."

"Isn't fifteen dollars a week a good deal for a child's nurse?" I asked.

"What do you pay a good stenographer?" he demanded.

"Why, a special one gets $20," I admitted. "But that work needs training and experience."

"So does taking care of babies!" he cried triumphantly. "Don't try to save on babies, Morton; it's poor economy."

I liked his point of view, and admired his family extremely. His wife was one of those sympathetic appreciative women who so help a man in his work. But the prospects of my own marriage seemed remote. That was why I was so glad of a good wholesome companionable friend like Dodo. We were so calmly intimate that I soon grew to discuss many of my ideas and plans with her. She was much interested in the figures given by my friend, and got me to set them all down for her.

He had twice my salary, and not a cent left at the year's end; and they were not in "society" either. Five hundred dollars was allowed for his personal expenses, and the same for her; little enough to dress on nowadays, he had assured me, with all amusements, travel, books and periodicals, and dentist bills, included.

"I don't think it ought to cost so much," said Dodo.

She was a business woman, and followed the figures closely; and of course she appreciated the high views I held on the subject, and my self-denial, too. I can't tell to this day how it happened; but before I knew it we were engaged. I was almost sorry, for a long engagement is a strain on both parties; but Dodo cheered me up; she said we were really no worse off than we were before, and in some ways better. At times I fully agreed with her.

So we drifted along for about a year, and then, after a good deal of distant discussion, we suddenly got married. I don't recall now just why we so hastily concluded to do it; I seemed to be in a kind of dream; but anyway we did, and were absurdly happy about it, too.

"Don't be a Goose, dear boy!" she said. "It isn't wicked to be married. And we're quite old enough!"

"But we can't afford it— you know we can't," I said. This was while we were camping out on our honey-vacation.

"Mr. Morton Howland," said my wife; "don't you worry one bit about affording it. I want you to understand that you've married a business woman."

"But you've given up your position!" I cried, aghast. "Surely, you don't think of going back!"

"I've given up one position," she replied with calmness, "and taken another. And I mean to fill it. Now you go peacefully on earning what you did before, and leave the housekeeping business to me— will you, Dear?"

Naturally I had to; for I couldn't keep house; even if I so desired I didn't know how. But I had read so much and heard so much and seen so much of the difficulties of housekeeping for young married people, that I confess I was a good deal worried. Toward the end of our trip I began to anticipate the burden of house-hunting. "About where do you think we are going to live?" I tentatively inquired.

"At 384 Meter Avenue," she promptly answered. I nearly dropped the paddle (we were canoeing at the moment), I was so astonished.

"That's a good location— for cheap flats," I said slowly. "Do you mean to say you've rented one, all by yourself?" She smiled comfortingly. Lovely teeth had my Dodo, strong and white and even, though not small.

"Not quite so bad as that, Dear," she answered, "but I've got the refusal. My friends the Scallens had it, and are moving out this Fall. It's a new building, they had it all papered very prettily, and if you like it we can move in as soon as they leave— say a week after moving time— it will be cheaper then. We'll look at it as soon as we return." We did. It seemed suitable enough; pleasant, and cheaper than I had thought possible. Indeed, I demurred a little on the question of style, and accessibility to friends; but Dodo said the people who really cared for us would come, and the people who did not could easily be spared.

We had married so hastily, right on the verge of vacation time, that I had hardly given a thought to furnishing but Dodo seemed to know just where to go and what to get; at much less cost than I had imagined. She produced $250 from her bank account, which she had been saving for years she said. I put up about the same; and we had that little flat as pretty and comfortable as any home I ever saw. She set her foot down about pictures though. "Time enough for those things when we can afford it," she said, and we certainly could not afford it then.

Then was materialized from some foreign clime a neat, strong young woman to do our house-work, washing and all. "She's an apprentice," said Dodo. "She is willing to learn housekeeping, and I am willing to teach her."

"How do you come to be so competent in house-work?" said I; "I thought you were a bookkeeper." Then Dodo smiled her large bright smile. "Morton, dear," she said, "I will now tell you a Secret! I have always intended to marry, and, as far as possible, I learned the business. I am a business woman, you know."

She certainly did know her business. She kept the household accounts like— well, like what she was— an expert accountant. When she furnished the kitchen she installed a good reliable set of weights and measures. She weighed the ice and the bread, she measured the milk and the potatoes, and made firm, definite, accurate protests when things went wrong; even sending samples of queer cream to the Board of Health for analysis. What with my business stationery and her accurate figures our letters were strangely potent, and we were well supplied, while our friends sadly and tamely complained of imposture and extortion.

Her largest item of expense in furnishing was a first-class sewing machine, and a marvelous female figure, made to measure, which stood in a corner and served as a "cloak tree" when not in use.

"You don't propose to make your own clothes, surely?" said I when this headless object appeared.

"Some of them," she admitted, "you'll see. Of course I can't dress for society."

Now I had prepared myself very conscientiously to meet the storms and shallows of early married life, as I had read about them; I was bound I would not bring home anybody to dinner without telephoning, and was prepared to assure my wife verbally, at least twice a day, that I loved her. She anticipated me on the dinner business, however.

"Look here!" she said, leading me to the pantry, when it was filled to her liking, and she showed me a special corner all marked off and labeled "For Emergencies." There was a whole outfit of eatables and drinkables in glass and tin.

"Now do your worst!" she said triumphantly. "You can bring home six men in the middle of the night— and I'll feed them! But you mustn't do it two nights in succession, for I'd have to stock up again."

As to tears and nervousness and "did I love her," I was almost, sometimes, a bit disappointed in Dodo, she was so calm. She was happy, and I was happy, but it seemed to require no effort at all. One morning I almost forgot, and left the elevator standing while I ran back to kiss her and say "I love you, dearest." She held me off from her with her two strong hands and laughed tenderly. "Dear boy!" she said, "I mean you shall."

I meditated on that all the way downtown. She meant I should. Well, I did. And the next time one of my new-married friends circuitously asked for a bit of light on what was to him a dark and perplexing question, I suddenly felt very light-hearted about my domestic affairs. Somehow we hadn't any troubles at all. Dodo kept well; we lived very comfortably and it cost far less than I had anticipated.

"How did you know how to train a servant?" I asked my wife.

"Dear," said she, "I have admitted to you that I always

intended to be married, when I found the man I could love and trust and honor." (Dodo overestimates my virtues, of course.)

"Lots of girls intend to marry," I interposed.

"Yes, I know they do," she agreed, "they want to love and be loved, but they don't learn their business! Now the business of house-work is not so abstruse nor so laborious, if you give your mind to it. I took an evening-course in domestic economy, read and studied some, and spent one vacation with an aunt of mine up in Vermont who 'does her own work.' The next vacation I did ours. I learned the trade in a small way."

We had a lovely time that first year. She dressed fairly well, but the smallness of her expense account was a standing marvel, owing to the machine and the Headless One.

"Did you take a course in dressmaking, too?" I inquired.

"Yes, in another vacation."

"You had the most industrious vacations of anyone I ever knew," said I, "and the most varied."

"I am no chicken, you see, my dear," was her cheerful reply, "and I like to work. You work, why shouldn't I?"

The only thing I had to criticize, if there was anything, was that Dodo wouldn't go to the theater and things like that, as often as I wanted her to. She said frankly that we couldn't afford it, and why should I want to go out for amusement when we had such a happy home? So we stayed at home a good deal, made a few calls, and played cards together, and were very happy, of course.

All this time I was in more or less anxiety lest that thousand dollar baby should descend upon us before we were ready, for I had only six hundred in the bank now. This dread event loomed awe-inspiringly on our horizon. I didn't say anything to Dodo about my fears, she must on no account be rendered anxious, but I lay awake nights and sometimes got up furtively and walked the floor in my room, thinking how I should raise the money.

She heard me one night. "Dear!" she called softly. "What are you doing? Is it burglars?" I reassured her on that point and she promptly reassured me on the other, as soon as she had made me tell her what I was worrying about.

"Why, bless you, dear," she said, serenely, "you needn't give a thought to that. I've got money in the bank for my baby."

"I thought you spent all of it for the furnishings," said I.

"Oh, that was the Furnishing Money! Cuddle down here, or you'll get cold, and I'll tell you all about it." So she explained in her calm strong cheerful way, with a little contented chuckle now and then, that she had always intended to be married.

"This is now no news," I exclaimed severely, "tell me something different."

"Well, in order to prepare for this Great Event," she went on, "I learned about housework, as you have seen. I saved money enough to furnish a small flat and put that in one bank. And I also anticipated this not Impossible Contingency and saved more money and put it in another bank!"

"Why two banks, if a mere man may inquire?"

"It is well," she replied sententiously, "not to have all one's eggs in one basket." I lay still and meditated on this new revelation.

"Have you got a thousand dollars, if this Remote Relative may so far urge for information?"

"I have just that sum," she replied.

"And, not to be impertinent, have you nine other thousands of dollars in nine other banks for nine other not Impossible Contingencies?"

She shook her head with determination. "Nine is an Impossible Contingency," she replied. "No, I have but one thousand dollars in this bank. Now you be good, and continue to practice your business, into the details of which I do not press, and let me carry on the Baby Business, which is mine."

It was a great load off my mind, and I slept well from that time on. So did Dodo. She kept well, busy, placid, and cheerful.

Once, I came home in a state of real terror. I had been learning, from one of my friends, and from books, of the terrible experience which lay before her. She saw that I was unusually intense in my affection and constantly regarded her with tender anxiety. "What is the matter with you, Morton?" said she.

"I'm— worried," I admitted. "I've been thinking— what if I should lose you! Oh Dodo! I'd rather have you than a thousand babies."

"I should think you would," said she calmly. "Now look here, Dear Boy! What are you worrying about? This is not an unusual enterprise I've embarked on; it's the plain course of nature, easily fulfilled by all manner of lady creatures! Don't you be afraid one bit, I'm not."

She wasn't. She kept her serene good cheer up to the last moment, had an efficient but inexpensive woman doctor, and soon was up again, still serene, with a Pink Person added to our family, of small size but of enormous importance.

Again I rather trembled for our peace and happiness, and mentally girded up my loins for wakeful nights of walking. No such troubles followed. We used separate rooms, and she kept the Pink Person in hers. Occasionally he made remarks in the night, but not for long. He was well, she was well— things went along very much as they did before.

I was "lost in wonder, love and praise" and especially in amazement at the continued cheapness of our living. Suddenly a thought struck me. "Where's the nurse?" I demanded.

"The nurse? Why she left long ago. I kept her only for the month."

"I mean the child's nurse," said I, "the fifteen dollar one."

"Oh— I'm the child's nurse," said Dodo.

"You!" said I. "Do you mean to say you take all the care of this child yourself?"

"Why, of course," said Dodo, "what's a mother for?"

"But— the time it takes," I protested, rather weakly.

"What do you expect me to do with my time, Morton?"

"Why, whatever you did before— This arrived."

"I will not have my son alluded to as 'This'!" said she severely. "Morton J. Hopkins, Jr., if you please. As to my time before? Why, I used it in preparing for time to come, of course. I have things ready for this youngster for three years ahead."

"How about the certified milk?" I asked.

Dodo smiled a superior smile; "I certify the milk," said she.

"Can you take care of the child and the house, too?"

"Bless you, Morton, 'the care' of a seven-room flat and a competent servant does not take more than an hour a day. And I shop while I'm out with the baby.

"Do you mean to say you are going to push the perambulator yourself?"

"Why not?" she asked a little sharply, "surely a mother need not be ashamed of the company of her own child."

"But you'll be taken for a nurse—"

"I am a nurse! And proud of it!"

I gazed at her in my third access of deep amazement. "Do you mean to say that you took lessons in child culture, too?"

"Too? Why, I took lessons in child culture first of all. How often must I tell you, Morton, that I always intended to be married!

Being married involves, to my mind, motherhood, that is what it is for! So naturally I prepared myself for the work I meant to do. I am a business woman, Morton, and this is my business."

That was twenty years ago. We have five children. Morton, Jr., is in college. So is Dorothea second. Dodo means to put them all through, she says. My salary has increased, but not so fast as prices, and neither of them so fast as my family. None of those babies cost a thousand dollars the first year though, nor five hundred thereafter; Dodo's thousand held out for the lot. We moved to a home in the suburbs, of course; that was only fair to the children. I live within my income always— we have but one servant still, and the children are all taught housework in the good old way.
None of my friends has as devoted, as vigorous and— and— as successful a wife as I have. She is the incarnate spirit of all the Housewives and House-mothers of history and fiction. The only thing I miss in her— if I must own to missing anything— is companionship and sympathy outside of household affairs.

My newspaper work— which she always calls "my business"— has remained a business. The literary aspirations I once had were long since laid aside as impracticable. And the only thing I miss in life beyond my home is, well— as a matter of fact, I don't have any life beyond my home— except, of course, my business. My friends are mostly co-commuters now. I couldn't keep up with the set I used to know. As my wife said, she couldn't dress for society, and, visibly, she couldn't.

We have few books, there isn't any margin for luxuries, she says; and of course we can't go to the plays and concerts in town. But these are unessentials— of course— as she says.

I am very proud of my home, my family, and my Amazing Dodo.

* * * * *

When I Was a Witch

Charlotte Gilman

Made in the USA
Columbia, SC
01 April 2019